After the Raid

After the Raid

CHRIS PALING

JONATHAN CAPE

LONDON

First published 1995

1 3 5 7 9 10 8 6 4 2

© Chris Paling 1995

Chris Paling has asserted his right
under the Copyright, Designs and Patents Act, 1988
to be identified as the author of this work

First published in the United Kingdom in 1995 by Jonathan Cape
Random House, 20 Vauxhall Bridge Road, London SW1V 2SA
Random House Australia (Pty) Limited
20 Alfred Street, Milsons Point, Sydney,
New South Wales 2061, Australia

Random House New Zealand Limited
18 Poland Road, Glenfield,
Auckland 10, New Zealand

Random House South Africa (Pty) Limited
PO Box 337, Bergvlei 2012, South Africa

Random House UK Limited Reg. No. 954009

A CIP catalogue record for this book
is available from the British Library

Papers used by Random House UK Limited are natural,
recyclable products made from wood grown in sustainable forests.
The manufacturing processes conform to the environmental
regulations of the country of origin.

ISBN 0-224-04114-2

Printed and bound in Great Britain by
Mackays of Chatham PLC

for Julie

. . . when I wak'd I cried to dream again.

The Tempest, Act III, scene ii

One

LONDON

THERE had been a raid the night before. On the way to Euston station, Gregory Swift's taxi was twice forced to detour past dark streets that had been hit in the bombardment. In one the face had been blown cleanly from a block of new flats so that only the fireplaces and hanging joists marked the original floors; now they looked like a tall ladder leaning against the back wall of the gutted building. In another, all that was left of an office building was the fragile metal skeleton of a liftshaft. The taxi driver said something and pointed towards the devastation, but Swift couldn't hear; the partition glass was closed and they were edging past a broken water main that was gushing loudly into the street. Swift saw a woman crying by a soot-blackened shop front; she was holding a pair of shoes for repair; beside her a young girl in a gaberdine mac was staring up at her, frightened, seeking reassurance, and Swift was even more glad to be leaving the city.

The traffic was halted behind a group of ARP

wardens remonstrating angrily with each other beside a cordoned hole in the road and a chalked sign which barred access to the public, warning of 'Gas'.

'Sorry, friend.' The taxi driver wearily slid back the partition without looking round.

'I can walk from here.' Swift leaned forward and paid the driver.

The driver said, 'You wouldn't mind if you could see a point in it.'

Swift was shocked by the man's defeatism. He felt that if he ceased to believe in the need for victory then he would cease to believe in anything. 'Oh, I'm sure I can see a point in it.' He continued the conversation with the back of the driver's bald head. It sat snugly in his brown scarf, slightly jaundiced, like an egg in an egg cup.

'Yeah. Bad night. That's all. When the amber went up I was up in Rotherhithe. Stupid. Lost all sense of time. Had to leave the cab in the open. Then I saw them come up the estuary . . .'

Swift had watched them too; he was firewatching on a department store roof. He had heard the drone and seen the heavy bombers locked in an unbroken grid as the searchlights reached for them through the broken clouds. The barrage balloons seemed to be tethered too low; the AA batteries barked angrily but ineffectually from the parks. And then from the docks came the orange glow beneath the mile-high sheet of smoke fuelled by oil and tar and rubber, as the sledge of metallic noise slid slowly from earshot. Then all that was left were the scattered shouts, the screams, whistles, sudden bells and the faces of the rescue squads sugared with sweat and frozen by the fires.

'Could be here for hours,' said the driver. 'Watch my back, will you.'

Swift stepped out into the busy street and waved the driver back with his rolled copy of *The Times*, then the cab was gone and the gap closed by a filthy black sedan. He joined a crocodile of schoolboys in green blazers, all bar one clutching gas masks. The exception, squat and overweight, kept breaking from the ranks to get a closer look at the bombed-out shops. Every so often he threw his arms wide and dive-bombed the neat squadron of his school-friends. The teacher looked back and admonished him with a snap of his fingers and the bark of his name.

'Arnold!'

'Sir.'

'Desist.'

'Sir.'

They peeled off down a side street, Arnold lagging, and Swift walked on to the station.

The concourse was crowded. He threaded his way towards the platform and picked up an early edition of the *Evening Standard* on the way. The front page detailed the losses of the night before and reported on the bravery in the face of the blitz.

The news was sober and, despite all that had happened to him over the previous week, Swift found it quietly reassuring. He rolled it around his morning paper and tucked them both beneath his arm.

He bought a ticket for Manchester; the train was already up on the board. By the entrance to the platform a young soldier, half hidden by a pile of kitbags, was vomiting noisily into a drain. A porter watched him unconcerned, his cap pushed at a jaunty angle to the back of his head. He consulted a watch on a long chain as though he was timing him. Swift walked on up the long train. He found a compartment with four empty seats in it and claimed two by sitting in one and placing his briefcase, newspaper and bowler hat on another. Then, almost as soon as he sat down, invisible threads of tiredness sealed his eyes and he was asleep.

*

When he awoke the train had broken from the suburbs and the countryside was cantering past, offering snapshots of railside paraphernalia and longer lagging views of hedges and hamlets. Only the far distance, the horizon gallowed by trees and the blue permanence of a river, seemed solid and safe and dependable.

A young woman was in the seat opposite and making no attempt to hide the fact that she had been looking at him. Swift looked away to save her embarrassment but felt compelled to study her reflection in the window; he could see she was still staring.

'You were snoring.' She weighed the statement evenly so that it became an observation and not a judgment.

Swift ignored the gambit. He had no desire to enter into a conversation that could potentially stretch the full distance from London to Manchester, so he maintained his intense study of the view rolling by the window. Someone had once told him always to travel facing backwards. The assertion was that the eyes grew less tired watching what had passed than trying always to focus on what was approaching. He realised that the observation did not hold true unless one's focus was fixed on the inside of the carriage, allowing only a peripheral glimpse of the exterior world.

Like a child he craned his neck to view the early afternoon sky: the clean clouds crosshatching the bright blue beyond. There was a small fighter plane just within sight; it seemed to be tailing the train. He caught the ghost of his face in the window; the reflection reminded him of who he was; for a moment he had lost himself entirely. He viewed his face with curiosity; the reflection softened the harsh planes of his features and the marble blue of his eyes. He was unshaven, the stubble shadowing his broad concave cheeks; his hair was worn unfashionably long at the back and swept straight back from his forehead. Swift was forty-one but his perpetual expression of scepticism allowed him to masquerade as an older man. In his presence people had an unremitting need to justify themselves even though he did not consciously court their justification.

'I wonder if he's deaf.' The woman turned to an imaginary companion. 'But then if he was deaf I don't imagine he would be blushing, would he.'

'It was the raid, last night. I couldn't sleep. I'm sorry my snoring disturbed you.' Swift tried to close off any further conversation by unrolling his newspapers and concentrating on the front page, but he had already given away more than he intended.

'What's your name?' The woman looked at him candidly; the question was little more than idle curiosity and Swift was irritated by the intrusion. In different times he would have brushed her off, but in different times the pretence of deafness would have been taken for what it was: a desire to be left alone. One of the early casualties of the blitz had been formality and Swift mourned its passing more than the loss of the irreplaceable churches and monuments. He conceded his reserve to her curiosity and let his paper drop to his knees. Before replying he considered the woman carefully. Her thin face was emotionless but not in repose; her eyes held the imprint of shock as she stared at him through wide pupils. She was what Swift imagined would be called 'fast'; her lipstick was bright, her bleached blonde hair showed black at the roots, but her Hampstead voice challenged the caricature.

'My name is Swift. Gregory Swift.'

'It doesn't suit you. I shall call you Mr Bowler.' She seemed to want to claim him by renaming him.

'Bowler? Oh, Bowler.' She was looking at his hat. 'Yes, I see.'

'You won't mind?'

'In the short time we shall be in each other's company no I shan't mind.'

'You're very kind to humour me. You have a kind face.'

'Thank you.'

'Oh, it wasn't a compliment. Men often misinterpret observations as compliments, don't they?'

'And compliments as observations?'

'Oh, hardly. Hardly.' She went back to her book, tacitly giving him permission to pick up his paper again.

The train had slowed; it clattered through a level crossing. Swift looked down, hoping now that the woman's curiosity had been satisfied. He saw two cars waiting to cross the line; the driver of the first was standing one foot on the road, the other on the running board, shirt-sleeved, watching the passing train with a broad grin. Behind the cars was a woman in an overall on a green tractor, gripping the wheel tight with thick sun-bronzed arms. A child on a tricycle idled at the edge of the road, bumping again and again into a fence post.

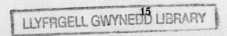

'Gregory.' The woman had put her book down again. She was trying the name for size.

Swift sighed heavily. 'Gregory. Yes.'

'I can't imagine ever calling a child Gregory. It's a grown-up name isn't it.'

By now Swift could distinguish other things about the woman, the skein of shell shock, the blankness and fear.

'And what do I call you?' he said.

'Why don't you guess?'

'Your name? I couldn't even begin . . .'

'It's Elaine. But try to guess my profession.'

'Yes, I would say — let me see.' He used up all of the permission she had given him to stare at her from head to toe. She had a compact body which she held straight like a bookend resisting the comfort of the contoured seat. Her blue mac was buttoned to the neck. Swift was surprised to feel the swell of a thrill when his eyes reached her ankles, which were perfect. She rocked her left shoe from high heel to toe; it was the sole conscious clue she offered to her sexuality, but it was one carefully chosen.

'A matron?' Swift enquired, although he was by now wondering whether the woman wasn't involved in the escort business.

'Hardly.' She laughed warmly and her voice found a lower register. 'Hardly.' Her hand went to her mouth, she was infected with the idea. Despite himself, Swift felt something cold and clean come into the compartment as though she had leant up and

16

opened the window; it swept through his heavy
heart displacing the coal dust and grief and cob-
webbed longings.

'Give me a clue.' He joined the game with a
sudden enthusiasm.

'You're very warm.'

'A nurse then. A nurse? Is that it?' He rose higher
to meet her mood.

'Yes Mr Bowler, a nurse — a nurse.' But the
sudden remembering of the rest of it dammed her
laugh and the glint in her grey eyes was dimmed
as suddenly as it had been lit.

'And are you a good nurse?' Swift was too late to
catch the change in her tone.

'A good nurse? No — good nurses don't let people
die, do they?'

The train stole into a tunnel, making conversation impossible.

'I'm sure it wasn't your fault,' he said when they
were out the other side. He was sober now, and
the weight of his understanding allowed him her
forgiveness though it was clear she had little to
spare for herself.

'Are you afraid to die?' She looked at him
candidly.

'What a question . . . Yes,' he said. 'Yes I am.'

'I'm not. I think it must be infectious: death.'

He said quickly, imagining that was what the
woman was asking of him, 'Oh, I'm sure you feel
that now . . .'

'No, I'm sorry. No, on that I am clear.' She flashed him a party smile. 'I think you have to be clear about something, don't you?'

She went back to her small blue book. Swift again took to looking out of the window, but his mind was too busy for reading. They were passing the dull orange chimneys and Victorian grandeur of a brick works. Life was resolutely going on but the significance of any of it had diminished beyond the tenuous lines of communication that had been established within the compartment. And that he found refreshing, having been for some time convinced that, like a persistent and debilitating illness, nothing could ever displace the greater significance of the war. Sometimes he even went as far as wondering whether, even when it ceased, anything ever would. But everything was changing; not just the rituals but the time scales. Courtship could be conducted in an evening, consummation, dissatisfaction and deceit condensed into a day.

'You mentioned dying,' he started.

'Yes?' She looked up, irritated that he'd disturbed her concentration.

'I think, I mean, this will probably sound ludicrous, especially, as it were, coming from a stranger . . .'

'Yes?' She coldly offered him no help towards further revelation.

'I suppose what I feel is that it's almost as if I've been afraid to live.'

'Then I'm sorry for you.' She made no effort to hide her disapproval.

'No, I wasn't asking for sympathy.'

'And I suppose you blame the war for that, do you?' Now she was sneering at him.

'Yes, I mean, I'm sure before the war...'

'You'd have been just the same. I know any number of people for whom the war is the most liberating thing that's ever happened to them. They've been released from the arduous responsibility towards happiness. The war has given them licence towards misery.'

'I see,' Swift said stiffly. 'Well I assure you I don't fall into that category.'

'Good.'

'And I resent your assumption that...'

'My, how you bristle, Mr Bowler, how you bristle.' She looked slyly at him, offering him shares in the stock of her greater understanding. He had shown his hand too early; he was out of practice and it annoyed him.

The train slowed as they arrived at a nondescript halt, the carriages jolting together as they slid to a stop at a platform full of soldiers. A rucksack slid into the compartment followed by a kitbag, a shout and a scrum of uniforms. Soon the air was choked with smoke and Swift resented the way they called him 'guv' when he asked whether they would mind him opening the window. To his surprise the nurse accepted a Senior Service one of the men offered her, but then he remembered that it was he who was the outsider and not she.

The men had finished basic training; they were full of boastful hope, explaining in detail their plans should they meet the Führer face to face. But the enemy was no more real to them than a cartoon army; paper thin, brought down so low by their ridicule that when they finally came to face them, their defeat would simply be a formality.

The woman operated expertly with the men, wresting the power from them after a short verbal tussle then picking them off individually, refusing to be swamped by the lusting khaki mass. Soon they were tamed, and when they got off Swift felt privileged to have watched the performance.

'Frightened, yes.' She picked up from where they had left off as if there had been no interlude in their conversation. 'I suppose we are, aren't we, I imagine we're living through something unique, I mean a nation being frightened. But it's what that fear does to you, that's the interesting thing isn't it.'

'Is it?'

'It is if you spend a little time considering it rather than simply feeling wretched.'

'I can't imagine any amount of consideration having an effect on being afraid; fear is not rational, is it?'

'Fear is ignorance, that's all.'

'Rubbish.' Swift launched in enthusiastically. 'How then do you explain the fear one feels during a raid. It's hardly ignorance, is it — in fact it's quite the opposite; it's clear that the fear lies in the threat of a bomb falling on you.'

'Or someone close to you.'

'Yes. Clearly. Clearly.' The woman's last remark jolted Swift back to the night of the raid; to the hour he had remained on the roof after the planes had dropped their bombs; to the hour he had watched the fires riot from street to street until it seemed that the whole city was alight. And then to the climb down the metal ladder into the attic above the department store, and the walk through the jumping shadows of the cavernous furniture showrooms backlit by the inferno outside; and then to the sweet sleep on the unmade bed, offered for sale by easy instalments — simply to delay the moment of arrival back at his home and finding it gone.

'Look — I'm going to stretch my legs,' he said. 'Will you keep an eye on my briefcase.'

'Of course.'

Swift opened the door of the compartment, then paused. 'By the way. That book.'

'Yes?'

'What is it?'

The train suddenly plunged into another tunnel and the din drowned her reply.

*

They had come to a stop at another small station.

21

Swift poked his head out of the window and called to the guard who was standing at the footplate talking to the driver.

'He can't hear me,' he reported, sighing as he settled back into his seat.

'Mm?' The woman closed her book and put it into her bag.

'He can't hear me: the guard. Or he doesn't want to hear me.'

'Why don't you get out then, and go and talk to him?'

'But the train may leave.'

'Don't be silly, if the guard's not on they'll hardly leave, will they?'

'Well I don't know,' Swift said tamely.

'Relax, it's a lovely day. Enjoy it.' She leant out of the window, releasing, as she did so, a waft of perfume from the folds of her coat. It was bitter, like gin, but barely concealed the heavier more solemn stench of disinfectant that clung to her from the wards. 'Lovely.' She turned her wrists to the sun. 'Did you see the flower bed?'

'What?'

'The flower bed — look, it's so pretty, all the geraniums are the same height like soldiers and they've whitewashed the stones round the edge.'

'Pretty?' It didn't look pretty to Swift, the freshly turned earth put him in mind of a grave.

'Look,' the woman said, 'he's coming now.'

The guard sauntered towards them, pausing at

the small station house to peer in through the windows. He then tried the door of the canopied ticket hall but it was locked.

'Why have we stopped?' Swift asked when the man reached them.

'Signal's against us, sir.'

'Yes, I assumed that, but why is it against us?'

'Blockage on the line. The driver reckons it could be a landslip.' The guard was no more than a youth; Swift was irritated by his habit of not meeting his eye.

'Well where are we?'

'Couldn't say. The nameplates have been taken down.'

The woman joined him at the window. 'That's a bit odd, I mean a train not knowing where it is.'

'We diverted down a branch line, must have been a reason for it.' Now the guard was facing two of them he was addressing all of his remarks to the woman through Swift. 'Get out, stretch your legs. I would.'

'Thank you. I will.'

'I think we'll be here some time.' The guard slouched off indolently towards his van to brew up.

'I'm meeting someone in Manchester. This is most inconvenient,' Swift said.

'Is it?' The woman was unsympathetic. 'I think we should do as the guard suggests and take the opportunity to look round.'

'But the train . . .'

'May leave. yes, but not without us I'm sure. Come on, be a gentleman, help me down.'

Swift stepped onto the long open space of the platform. There were two identical flower beds, one on each side of the ticket office; the platform was separated from the narrow lane behind by a white picket fence. Apart from a black metal chest, two stacked wicker pigeon baskets, a porter's trolley and a bucket of sand, there was little to indicate that the station was in use.

The woman led the way towards the ticket hall along the carriages that were now punctuated with heads leaning from the windows. Swift dawdled, not wanting the train to leave without him. He watched the woman disappear inside the hall as scattered travellers stepped gingerly onto the platform like skaters onto a freshly frozen lake. Between them swooped a young boy with outstretched arms machine-gunning the stragglers. He came to a halt in front of Swift.

'Oh,' said the boy.

Swift recognised him immediately. 'It's Arnold, isn't it?'

'Yes, sir. How did you know, sir?'

'I saw you. By Euston, you and your school-friends.'

'Have you seen them, sir?'

'No, no I haven't. Are they not on the train with you?'

'We got split up. I think I may be lost.' He jabbed

a finger to his eye and began rubbing it. He seemed to be trying to hold back tears.

'Well, they must be somewhere around, mustn't they?'

'Yes sir, I suppose they must.'

'Well, why don't you look for them and if you can't find them come back to me and I'll see what I can do to help.' Swift had no intention of helping but he felt honour bound to make the offer.

'Yes, thank you, sir.' Arnold began walking away solemnly. 'I don't suppose you've seen my gas mask, sir?'

'On the train you mean?'

'Anywhere really.' His mouth was a sudden smudge of red, his blue eyes turned from pensiveness to pain. 'I didn't mean to lose it. I really didn't mean to.' He wandered away stubbing his toes; the woman passed him on her way back up the platform.

'Come with me,' she commanded, holding her hand out to Swift who took it unquestioningly. She then led him towards the ticket hall. 'I'm not going in there alone, I don't like it.'

'What do you mean?'

'I just don't like it.'

'Then don't go in.'

'I want to go in.'

They passed circles of strangers widening as more travellers stepped from the train. For a while it seemed they had allowed each other the permission to be excused the formalities of introduction. An air of repressed jollity was slowly pervading the platform; occasionally a laugh would cannon from one group to the next, setting up a chain reaction of guilty pleasure.

Swift tried the door of the ticket hall. 'It's locked.'

'No it's not.' The woman turned the knob the other way and stepped in. The door swung shut behind them. 'God, it's as cold as a cave in here.' Her breath billowed into the old air; she hugged herself; Swift felt the room stealing his warmth.

'I shouldn't think this room has been open for years.' He traced a finger along the dust on the mantelpiece. The bright posters offering travel to the Cornish Riviera belonged to a different era.

The woman was at the counter which a half pulled roller blind indicated was 'closed'. 'I love old stations, don't you?'

'Well no, not particularly.'

'God, I do. The coal dust on the platform, the soft eccentric smells of summer. So many possibilities.'

'I really do think we should go back to the platform.'

'Why? You must take every opportunity to pause, take stock, make decisions about your life; don't always let others do it for you.'

Swift was becoming increasingly concerned for the woman's sanity. But he felt an interest in her which prevented him from simply telling her to mind her own business. 'And what makes you think I'm not guided by my own decisions?'

'Look at you.'

'Are you always this rude to strangers or have you singled me out for special attention?'

'Oh, I don't think of you as a stranger. Anyway, I only offer advice to people I like.' They were circling each other, conversing while directing their attention towards what the sparse room offered them.

'That's most gratifying.'

They came face to face; the woman laughed. 'God, you're so stiff. Stiff. Stiff. Stiff!' She punctuated the repeated accusation by punching him lightly in the chest.

Swift snapped. He could bear her intrusive observations, he had been flattered by her attention and he felt a very real attraction towards the woman, but the sudden physical contact was too much. 'Don't do that.' He took her wrist firmly and held it tightly.

She stared hard into his face trying to read what he was feeling. His reaction had shocked but not entirely displeased her; it indicated a strength she had almost been convinced he did not possess and there was nothing she despised more than weakness.

'I'm sorry.' There was enough arrogance in the apology for her to salvage her pride but not sufficient for him to press her harder.

Swift dropped her wrist. 'No, I'm sorry.' The gentleness was gone from his voice.

'I got you wrong, didn't I?' she said.

'Yes. Give me a cigarette will you.'

She retrieved the packet elegantly from the bag and they sat side by side on the wooden bench beside the counter, intimate and silent as though they had just made love.

'I thought you were a tart.' Swift broke the silence.

'That's nice.'

'Only at the beginning.'

'And now?'

'I got you wrong too, didn't I?'

'Yes.'

The woman stood and stubbed her cigarette out with the toe of her shoe. 'I think I'll have a look outside. I can't stand being locked in. Come with me.' She held out her hand, and when Swift did not take it, she translated the movement to a busying with the clasp of her handbag.

'I don't want to be stranded here if the train leaves,' he said.

'It won't leave, but if you're concerned why don't you go and check with the guard?'

Swift finished his cigarette then walked back onto the now crowded platform and found the guard drinking tea with the driver.

'Any news?'

'We won't be off yet.'

'Is there nothing we can do?'

'Nothing . . . Sorry.' The apology was twisted into

an insult. Calmness had descended on the two men; the holiday spirit of the workman released for a week from the timetable and punch card.

'Will you give me some signal when you intend to leave?'

'We'll blow the whistle. Don't worry, we won't leave without you, sir.'

The men exchanged a private smile. Swift knew he was the butt of their joke but there was little he could salvage from the situation. As he walked back towards the waiting-room he heard them laugh. As he reached the door Arnold breathlessly caught up with him.

'Can't find them, sir.'

'Oh.' Swift had forgotten about Arnold. 'Look, are you sure they were on the train?'

'Oh yes, sir. Absolutely, sir.'

'In that case I don't see ... Oh, come in, we'll find them later.'

Swift tried the door of the waiting-room but it was locked.

'Here sir.' Arnold turned the knob easily and led the way in. 'Crikey!'

'What?' Swift said irritably.

'Is it haunted do you think?'

'I don't imagine so. Look, can I come in please?'

'Oh yes, sorry sir.' Arnold moved aside to let Swift through the door.

'And for God's sake,' Swift snapped, 'stop calling me sir. I'm not your bloody teacher.'

'Oh, right. Bloody right, sir.'

The room was empty but Swift heard a movement in the next room; a sign over the door announced it to be the 'Ladies Waiting-Room'. He stood by the door and listened.

'What is it?' Arnold asked.

'Shut up.' Swift pressed his ear to the door. It gave a little. There was a sudden loud slap from behind him. Swift span round. Arnold was gone. Swift's heart began to race.

'Tickets please, sir.'

'For God's sake!' The boy was behind the glass of the ticket hatch; only the top half of his face showed over the counter: two small round eyes and a porcine nose set beneath a thick forehead. A black peaked cap hid his inelegant basin haircut. The slap was the sound of the blind rolling up.

'Will you come out of there, you bloody imbecile!'

The face and its sudden look of hurt disappeared and as it did so the Ladies Room door opened and the woman walked out. She had been crying; the powder was smudged on her cheeks.

'Hello.' Arnold greeted the woman warmly, Swift's admonishment already forgotten.

'A boy,' said the woman sadly.

'Yes,' said Swift. 'He's lost his party. I said he could . . . look, are you all right?'

'Yes.' She sat at the bench by the counter and rummaged for her cigarettes.

'Are you sure?'

'Quite sure. It's just that . . . things get a little too much sometimes. You can understand that, can't you?'

'Of course. Of course.'

The train whistled shrilly. Swift jumped. Almost immediately the carriages began to move past the window.

He leapt for the door but it was jammed.

'Here sir!' Arnold turned the knob the other way and darted past him onto the platform. The train was picking up speed; the carriage windows were lined with faces looking down at them. The faces began to blur and Swift knew there was already nothing he could do, so he stopped and stared as the last carriage flashed past and the station settled once more to silence, broken only by Arnold's sad snuffling and the resumption of birdsong.

*

Swift took Arnold back into the waiting-room. The woman held her hand out to the boy, he took it and she pulled him to her; her coat muffled his tears. 'Poor little lamb.'

'This could be serious,' Swift said gravely.

'And why is that, Mr Bowler?' Something of her early sureness had returned.

'Because for one thing this was not a scheduled stop, and for another we could be miles from anywhere.'

31

'That sounds like part and parcel of the same problem to me.'

'I must say I find your glibness less than refreshing.'

'That was rather a mouthful, wasn't it? Now loosen your tie and relax.'

'I don't want to relax, I don't feel relaxed.'

'Well go and take your temper out on somebody else, the boy is upset and you're really not helping.'

Arnold's sobbing slowly subsided. The woman gave him her handkerchief and he filled it gratefully and noisily. She was looking at the boy fondly. Swift began to feel profoundly uneasy; there was now a bond between Arnold and the woman that already excluded him. It had been forged the moment they had set eyes on each other; like a game of charades Swift felt they were holding the answer and would reveal the truth of it only when he arrived at it himself.

*

The three of them walked out between the empty milk churns into the sunny narrow lane behind the station — Arnold first, small and rotund like a barrel on a milking stool, then Swift, falling into step on his left, and as he did so becoming intrigued by his air of porcine elegance; his thick pink neck shorn redly of its hair, his constant gruntings and animal exuberance. Swift had never had much time for children. On Arnold's right, the woman walked half a step ahead, having tacitly taken the lead of the expedition. She glided rather than walked along the parched road, her head level and unmoving on a delicate neck, her eyes fixed on a point in the distance, unblinking; evangelical.

The unmetalled lane, mazed between tall bramble hedges, led them to a verged crossroads; a wooden bench offered the opportunity to rest, but the woman pressed on, choosing not to deviate from their route. Swift glanced left and right at the two other options; both vanished into bends at almost exactly the same point. He loosened his tie, then took it off and put it in his pocket. Arnold took his hand and he accepted the clamminess uneasily, but soon, in the silence that lay across the three of them, began to take comfort from it. The heat of the afternoon closed further in on them and Arnold began to emanate an aroma like a pile of grass steaming gently in the sun. Swift saw that the woman had taken Arnold's other hand and they had fallen into step.

The bramble hedge was finally broken by a fence, they paused to look across a field which slanted down to a river. The railway line shadowed the far bank and then vanished into a cutting.

'I wonder if we're going the right way,' Swift said.

'Do you?' said the woman.

'I wonder if we should have turned off at the crossroads.'

'I wonder,' the woman mimicked.

'I don't think there's any need to be rude, do you?'

'I'm not being rude.' She sat on the squat earth bank into which the fence posts were sunk and began fanning herself with her hand. Arnold clambered with surprising agility over the fence. 'Won't be long,' he said and dribbled an imaginary football down towards the river.

'I just wonder if you don't say things for the sake of it, that's all.' The woman was lighting another cigarette.

'Like what?' The heat was adding to Swift's irritation, he felt light-headed and disorientated.

'Like "I wonder if we should have turned left." If you want to lead the way then do, I won't mind.'

'I don't want to lead the way, that's not the point,' Swift said sulkily. 'I don't . . . I mean, I suppose what I mean is that I don't understand you, that's all. I can't somehow make you out.'

'And why do you need to "make me out"?'

'I thought,' he began, '. . . on the train, well . . .'

'Well what?' she said sharply.

'Well, that we seemed to have hit it off.'

'We did.'

'But now, well, as I said, I just can't make you out, that's all.'

'Are you married, Mr Bowler?' The question was loaded with spite.

'Yes, no. I mean yes, I was, but I suppose I'm not now.'

34

'You suppose you're not. I wonder how you can suppose you're not. Aren't you sure?'

Swift turned away and leant a foot on the bottom rung of the wooden fence. Arnold had reached the river, he was scuffing stones off the riverbank. 'She was killed in a raid.'

The woman drew in her knees like a child and rested her chin on them. She pulled hard on her cigarette. 'I'm sorry.' The apology was exhaled with the smoke.

'It was just . . . anyway, they bloody blew half of the terrace away. She should have been in the shelter, that was the point, but, I don't know, that's how it was.'

'I'm sorry.' Her second apology had a wider compass.

'Strange as it may sound, it didn't touch me much — not then — I was out firewatching. I missed all of the . . . you know, anyway I saw the street go from my roof. It was a hell of a night . . . hell of a night.'

'Yes . . . but I thought, you see,' the woman said slowly, 'that you were married and you were just trying to pick me up. You look like the sort, that's all. You can't blame me.'

'Oh, I don't blame you. I really don't. I wonder if we should call him back, I'd hate him to fall in and drown.'

Arnold was balancing on one foot and leaning at a perilous angle over the bank.

35

'He'll be all right.' The woman didn't look round. 'I suppose I felt quite flattered really.'

'Did you?'

'That you showed an interest in me.'

'That can hardly be an uncommon experience for a woman like you.'

'You'd be surprised. You really would.'

'Enlighten me then.'

The woman laughed self-consciously and scrambled to her feet. 'You don't ask questions like that.'

'Don't I?' He saw she was blushing and stored the question for later, then gave way to a sudden irrational impulse and climbed over the fence. He felt light and young. He knew both the woman and Arnold were watching him, and on another whim he took off his bowler hat and threw it as hard as he could towards the river. It landed upside down and bobbed as the current snatched it away. Arnold stared, Swift heard the woman call encouragement and he broke into a run, picking up speed down the incline. He slowed to a walk when he realised how ludicrous he must look and reached the boy on the bank elated and embarrassed.

'It's all right.' Arnold understood; he seemed to have aged five years since the station. 'But you've lost your hat.'

They watched it race away, twisting and bumping like a dodgem as it hit a half-submerged branch, then righting itself as though it had a sense of its ultimate destination.

'Do you swim?' Swift peered down at the complex currents.

'No, I'd like to,' the boy said eagerly.

'You should learn: get your father to teach you.'

'They'll teach us at school. I should think school is the best place to learn things like swimming.' Arnold had borrowed the phrase but not the conviction with which it had originally been used.

'And will they?'

'Will they what?'

'Teach you to swim.'

'Oh, I'm sure they will. There's a public pool quite close to the school. We drove past it once, my father and I, but my father said it was a haven for diseased feet. I don't think he was keen that we should go in.'

'I can imagine not. What do you think of Elaine?'

'She's like matron really.'

'Not your mother?'

'No. Matron.'

'Do you see your mother and father much?'

'In the vacs, sometimes in the vacs,' Arnold said vaguely. 'I'm starving, do you think we'll find something to eat soon?'

'Are you ready?'

'Yes.'

'Come on then.'

The boy led the way back up the field, but when they reached the fence they discovered the woman had gone.

Swift and Arnold continued down the lane, eventually passing an empty cottage and a cluster of buildings and barns which seemed to mark a distant outpost of a large farm. Swift was tired; he was conscious he was holding the boy back in his quest for food. Arnold was diverting what was left of his energy to scouting ahead round blind bends, then rushing back to report what he'd discovered so that when they reached them Swift found it was with a distinct sense of déjà vu.

They came to another wooden bench, standing by a pond which was drying up by degrees. Swift sat tiredly and removed his jacket. 'Look, Arnold.'

'Yes sir.'

'I'm fagged out. Why don't you go on; we can't be far from the village now.'

'You'll be all right, sir?'

Swift laughed. 'I'll be all right. Go on, shoo.' He waved the boy away, lay on the bench, closed his eyes and slept.

'MANCHESTER, sir. Manchester.'

Swift felt his shoulder being shaken, he opened his eyes and blinked them clear. 'What did you say?'

'Manchester London Road,' the porter said. 'Are you all right?'

'Yes. Yes, I'm fine.' Swift stood unsteadily; he felt light-headed and a little sick, as though he'd just leapt from a spinning playground roundabout. He collected his briefcase and stepped down onto the platform.

The unfamiliar station was teeming with travellers, streaming from the waiting trains. A lighted flower stall stood on the echoing concourse, diverting the human flow like a stepping stone in a stream. Suddenly Swift was being hugged by a woman, a head shorter than he was, but strong and hard-bodied so that the contact yielded little in the way of comfort. Her hair smelt strongly of lavender.

'I'm so, so, sorry, but you look so . . . well, I don't suppose it's hit you yet. God, I'm so sorry.' She took him fiercely by the hand and steered him through the crowds towards the front of the station. Outside, night was falling and the air carried a sharp chill.

'We'll get you back. Patrick's at home, he's terribly . . . well, we all are of course. Look, how are you *really*?'

They stopped beside a short line of taxis. The woman took his shoulders and looked at him critically as though she was examining a canvas for cracks.

'I don't know, Dorothy. I think I may be going mad.'

'We shall forgive you anything, Gregory. Come and be mad with us for a while.'

'Yes, I think I would like that.' Swift folded himself into the back seat of the cab, the woman gave sharp instructions to the driver and they pulled into the light traffic. Swift looked at his sister and she smiled back reassuringly.

'It's been a long time, hasn't it?' he said.

'It's only when something like this happens that time seems to have any meaning. Life goes on and then another year has passed, and you know it's time you'll never have again. We've never been good at making time for each other, have we?'

'Perhaps we don't need to,' Swift said with discomfort.

'Perhaps.'

'I mean we always pick up where we've left off.'

'I should like to think that was the case, Gregory,

but then life has a habit of getting between us, doesn't it?'

They had begun the old game of apportioning the blame for their estrangement on each other.

'Oh, I suppose it's not important anyway.' Swift hadn't the heart for a fight, particularly with his sister who knew exactly how to raise the stakes between them.

'No, please go on.' Dorothy took his cold hand and cradled it in her lap; it was the moment when, as a child, she would have cried 'Pax!' and crossed her fingers.

'I just feel with you I don't have to explain, that's all,' Swift said dully.

'Of course you don't.' She squeezed his hand but Swift missed her look of concern; he was looking up above the tall ramparts of the city, waiting for the ululations of the sirens signalling the start of another night of hell.

Patrick welcomed him to their well-appointed semi on the outskirts of the city. This is the England we're fighting for, Swift thought as he surveyed the neat box hedges in the front garden. His brother-in-law had gone reassuringly grey.

'Come in, my friend. Come in,' Patrick said in his ground bass and drew him in like a preacher. Two teenage boys in shorts, white shirts and ties stood uncomfortably at attention by the living-room door. The younger one was unquestionably his sister's boy: bright, dark-haired and thin-lipped with challenging eyes and an expression that teetered on the edge of insolence. The older one clearly borrowed heavily from Patrick's line: broad and open-faced, clearly a 'good chap' destined to spend his life misinterpreting and misunderstanding the complications of his fellow men. But women would forgive him and love him for his simplicity, and, in so doing, he would live a charmed and happy life.

'Hello, Uncle Gregory.' The older boy marched forward one step, his hand outstretched in a formal welcome.

'Haven't you got a kiss for me?' he said, then they were both on him, one under each shoulder, and Swift remembered how he used to wheel them round when they were babies and they would squeal with glee.

'All right boys.' His sister gave a pre-arranged signal and they left the adults to their grown-up world of pain and loss.

'Sit down. Sit down.' Patrick papered over the silence and moved a chair by the empty fireplace. 'I could rustle up a Scotch if you'd care for one.'

'Could you?' said Swift.

'Mum's the word.' Patrick tapped his nose and went to fetch the glasses.

'Are you all right?' Dorothy looked at him carefully, wanting a progress report. Swift took the armchair Patrick had offered.

'The strangest thing is . . . I really don't know.'

Dorothy sat in the chair facing him. 'Do you feel ill?'

'Just a little ... giddy. I slept on the train and when I woke ... well, perhaps I am sickening for something.'

Dorothy went to him and placed a hand on his forehead. 'You don't feel hot.'

'No. No, I suppose I don't.'

'Here you are, old man.' Patrick blustered in and distributed a patently pre-prepared tray of drinks. Dorothy silenced him with a glance and, after closing the floral curtains, he found an excuse to do something upstairs.

Swift sipped at the minuscule measure of whisky. 'It's almost as if the raid was a year ago.'

'Shock, I imagine.' Dorothy was perched on the edge of her chair trying vainly to read his face for signs of incipient insanity.

'But, I mean, when was it? You know I really can't remember.'

'Perhaps it would be best not to discuss it.'

'Why not?' he said sharply.

'I thought, Gregory, perhaps you'd rather get settled in first. Have dinner, there's no need to rush, is there?' She was so much like their mother.

'Well, you always did know best, didn't you, Dorothy?' Swift stood angrily. 'Will you show me to my room please.'

'Yes, of course,' she said in a voice which offered

him conditional forgiveness for his outburst. '. . . Look, why don't you sit down.'

Swift sat, realising he still had his coat on.

'You do know really, don't you?' It was almost a plea to his better nature.

'Know?'

'About what happened.'

'Yes, I'm sure I know, I just can't seem to recall the details.'

'All right. Shall I tell you?'

'Yes.'

'It was six days ago according to your telegram.'

'Six days?'

'Yes. The funeral was two days ago.'

'Of course it was.'

Swift could see the church: the darkness hanging in folds like heavy fabric from the rafters, the sun slanting through the small windows, the dust on the pews from the H. E. that had cratered the graveyard, and the vicar making a hash of his sermon; a clumsy reference to the destruction of St Giles in Cripplegate, a picture of a woman that wasn't his wife.

'You asked us not to come because you didn't want the boys . . . well, you know all that, don't you?'

'Of course.'

'And that's almost as much as we know. "Details to follow," that's what you said.'

'Yes, I remember. I don't suppose there's any chance of a fire in the grate is there?'

'We're trying to save on wood, but if you're cold . . .'

'I can't seem to get warm at all. Especially at night.'

'No, I know how you must feel. Sometimes when Patrick's away . . . but then I know he's coming back, don't I, so I suppose . . . Oh, God, Gregory. Oh God!' She cried stiffly into her palm, whether for herself or for him Swift was unsure. As always they were separated by the years that lay between them as brother and sister. She had never entirely forgiven him for being the elder and brighter, he couldn't forgive her for being younger and more dependent. Even now it still seemed to matter, though the objects of their competing affections were long dead.

Swift wanted to comfort his sister but he knew she would never forgive him if he did. Even at the funeral of their mother they had cried alone.

'You mustn't feel sorry for me,' he said. 'I don't entirely feel sorry for myself, you know.'

'Perhaps that's why I do. Look, let's have a fire. I'll get the boys to fetch some wood in.'

'It really doesn't matter.'

'Nonsense. Then when it's lit we can eat in here; it will make a change.' She stood and brushed invisible crumbs from her lap. 'Take your coat off. I'll check on the dinner.'

She left him in the unwelcoming room with its unhappy collision of heavily patterned fabrics and big, new furniture. The radiogram was silent, the curtains closed and there was nothing left in his glass to entertain him, so Swift took the opportunity for a brief nap.

*

A boy was standing by him when he woke. 'Arnold, what's up ahead?' he said.

'It's Tom. Not Arnold,' said the younger of his sister's sons.

'Tom! Of course it is. What on earth am I . . .'

'Mother says dinner is nearly ready, she wonders if you wouldn't like to go up and wash.'

'I will. Thank you.'

'Is that all right?' The boy began edging towards the door.

'Yes. It's all right.'

Swift found the upstairs bathroom and splashed cold water on his face. The expression that confronted him in the small mirror was one of total bemusement. He then took his briefcase into the guest room where he realised that he hadn't brought any clothes with him and the realisation broke open a crack in his memories of the night of the raid. He sat on the bed and found himself staring at the rubble of his house as a group of men picked through the carpet of debris.

'Won't be long now.' A black-hatted warden was

beside him. Swift felt the man's hand go to his shoulder.

'I suppose there's no hope?'

'Oh, there's always hope. Always.' The man's face was grained with dirt; he threw a heavy grey blanket round his shoulders. Swift was holding a chipped tin mug of sweet tea. It was all wrong: the dimensions of the street were wrong, he was standing facing what should have been his front door but looking directly at his back garden wall. The Anderson shelter squatted by the potato patch untouched by the explosion.

'I suppose you see this all the time,' said Swift.

'Pretty much every night now. It doesn't make it any easier you know,' he added hurriedly.

'I wasn't suggesting that it did.' The significance of the war and the smallness of Swift's own life came back to him. On the larger canvas of human suffering he felt he had barely rated representation. Death and life were always grander; carried out with more panache and vigour elsewhere.

'Over here!' One of the stooped men picking through the wreckage waved them over. It was the signal for the other men to stop, draw breath, and lean on their shovels. All eyes turned to Swift as the strong hand of the warden guided him over the debris.

'I'm sorry, you'll have to wait.' Swift paused and drew three deep breaths. He felt the night press down on him; a note rang in his head like a tuning fork held to his skull. Then his heart and his head meshed to meet the mood of the moment and, thus prepared, he allowed himself to be led forward. The searcher's eyes stayed on his face as he forced himself to contemplate what lay at the man's feet.

'No, no, that's not her,' he said with relief. 'She has fair hair.' Gently the searcher leant down and brushed the dust aside. Swift was suddenly glad of the hand on his arm even though it could not prevent him from dropping to his knees.

Death had surprised the small face in the rubble. Those features that remained bore a frozen look of shock. The rest had been pulped to red and black and coated with a crust of grey dust like a layer of mould on a jar of jam.

*

'So there you are.' Dorothy came into Swift's room and closed the door behind her. 'Don't you want the light on?'

'No. Not really.'

She sat beside him on the bed. 'We've had dinner. Patrick said we should leave you to come down when you were ready.'

'Good of him. Good of you I mean.'

'Would you like to come down now?'

'Soon, I think.' Swift stared out of the window at the starless sky. 'I don't think I could eat.'

'Please do whatever you want, Gregory.'

'I feel so wretched. I feel so wretched for not remembering.'

'You will remember.'

'Oh, I remember now. Some of it.'

'Do you?' She looked at him with curiosity.

'It was the ... the suddenness of space, as if the street had been swept away by a huge brush. But it had been done so carelessly that nobody had troubled to sort the people from the buildings. Carelessness though, I suppose that's what I felt. It didn't seem possible that anybody could have planned cold-bloodedly to target my street. Mm?'

'I suppose you would ...'

'I mean,' Swift pressed on, 'if they flattened your house tonight you'd be hard pushed to believe that Air Marshal Goering had conferred with his bomber pilots and said, "Tonight you bomb Patrick and Dorothy — and you bomb Paul and Eloise" — you see? So you have to believe it is carelessness, which of course begs the question where did they intend to ... Oh God, I think I must have some air.' He moved to the door and opened it; the light from the landing spilled into the room.

'Shall I come?' Dorothy said.

'No thank you.'

'I'll send one of the boys with you.'

'Strictly not necessary. I'd just like to walk round the block to clear my head.'

'Don't get cold.'

'No.'

Swift walked the length of the street. He picked his way carefully along the pavement; no lights were showing and the half moon threw only a little luminous light at the streets. A car went past with sinister masked headlights, then a warden cycled by and called a cheery greeting. The road ended and gave onto a patch of open ground marked by the silhouettes of allotment trellises and bean poles. They looked like the masts and rigging of small boats bobbing in a land-locked harbour. Some of the plots boasted sheds which showed as oblong stains in the blue black. Swift picked his way between vegetable patches to reach a large shed; it was a railway carriage supported by piles of house bricks. He tried each door along its length until he came to one which opened. He stepped into the darkness which smelt of lime and compost, stumbled on a sieve and picked his way to a place free of clutter where he lowered himself down into the earthy warmth.

THE HOSPITAL

A FLY woke him from a luxurious sleep. It flew at his nose, landed, then flew off again before returning to settle on his cheek. Swift waved it away without opening his eyes and it buzzed slowly away into the lush perspective of a summer skyline. The sleep on Swift's lips tasted sweet; the sun lay across him like a crisp cotton sheet; he had an immense feeling of well-being that he clearly remembered experiencing only once before when, as a small child, he was allowed to wander naked across a secluded dune towards the sea. He was constrained by nothing, he feared nothing and the world was simply a place populated by people who towered over him, occasionally reaching down smiling to lift him up. And the only pain he felt was the delicious pain of love for his mother who lay on a tartan rug prepared to assent to his tiniest demand.

He lay awake with no desire to open his eyes. A tennis game occupied the space in the left distance, the players were either knocking up or pursuing each point so unstrenuously that the ball seemed always to be in play, singing from one of the high-strung racquets only to pop on the grass and sing back again in strict waltz time.

'One hundred!' a young girl's voice exclaimed excitedly.

'Quiet, I know. Quiet, just concentrate.' It was another girl, little distinguished from the first except by the solemnity with which she was pursuing her target.

'I think I'm going to laugh!' the first girl said.

'Stupid. Stupid! Don't laugh, think of something awful.'

'No I won't!' The ball bounced and was not returned. Swift opened an eye. The receiver was standing with her arms crossed looking petulantly at the server who was sucking the ribbon which hung from her wide-brimmed straw sun hat.

'Stupid. You always spoil it,' the more severe girl said.

'You do.'

'Oh grow up, child. Do grow up.' The girl flounced off in a long loose dress that softened her angry movements. She was nearly a woman, some five or so years older than the other girl. All she had left to lose was her uncertainty. The younger girl watched her go; Swift felt that she was seeing the same things in her companion as he was. She had all but lost her.

Swift saw that he was in a garden. It was unfamiliar. An old crumbling orange wall marked the far boundary of the court. The net was loose and holed, the lines overgrown. Behind it the steep planes of the roof of a large house showed, to the left a lawn and beyond that a line of saplings shimmered in the heat haze like a watercolour on a sail. Swift was protected from the full glare of the fierce sun by the low boughs of a cedar tree. He was lying on a wooden bench and the younger girl was walking slowly towards him, dragging her toes through the long grass, greening her white shoes.

'One hundred and five.' The girl sat beside Swift so that he was forced to hunch up his legs. They felt stiff and unused. 'Can I have a drink?' Swift sat up; a circular metal table beside the bench held a water jug covered with a sheet of thick white paper. Two empty glasses were upturned beside it. Swift poured the girl a drink; tiny bubbles raced and glittered as the clear water filled the glass. 'Feel me, I'm baking.' The girl held back her fringe, Swift felt her forehead. 'Yes, you are.'

'Would you like to play?'

Swift said, 'I'm sorry, I'm hardly dressed for tennis,' but looking down he saw that he was. He was wearing a pair of cricket flannels and an open-necked white cotton shirt. A straw hat lay by the seat next to a tennis racquet. 'All right then. One hundred and five. We'll try to beat it, shall we? Only you mustn't laugh.'

'I promise.' The child took his hand and led him through the grass. 'Will you be here much longer?'

'I don't know. We'll see.'

'I hope you are. You serve.'

They had reached the net, the girl bounded to the left baseline, Swift took his place, squared himself to face her, then served underarm.

'Good serve!' the small voice called enthusiastically. They synchronised their games, Swift took each return on his backhand, the girl, her face masked in concentration, her tongue clamped between her teeth, took each of his backhands on her forehand. After two false starts they reached a hundred, then a hundred and twenty and Swift ceased counting. The rhythm was finally broken only when a woman appeared through a gap in the orange wall.

'Two hundred and six!' the girl called. 'I'll serve.'

'Wait. I need a rest.' Swift lowered himself stiffly to the ground using his racquet as a crutch.

'Boring.' The girl began a solitary game of batting the ball into the air on the horizontal face of the racquet.

'You're up then.' The woman came over to him, then knelt and snapped a long blade of grass. She smelt faintly of sweat.

'Up? Yes, I suppose I am.' Swift said.

'Don't let me stop you.' The woman was immediately irritated by Swift's unenthusiastic response. She was early middle aged, untidily dressed with a ragged greasy fringe falling like a curtain over her wounded eyes.

'Oh, you're not. We're resting between rallies.' He managed a hospitable smile.

'Will you be eating anything?'

'Now?'

'No. Not now. Tonight.' The woman seemed to be working hard at controlling her anger. Swift felt he was annoying her without knowing why. Too many questions occurred to him for him to embark on asking any of them. The sole imperative he did have was to return to the rally.

'They have to know. For the numbers,' the woman pressed. She looked at him heavily as though he had already transgressed 'their' rules.

'Is this a hospital?' Swift said with inspiration.

'Oh God! Oh God.' The woman laughed with joyous cruelty. 'What did you think it was?'

'I really wasn't sure.'

'You people ... you people.' He bore the dull weight of her broad accusation. She had now devoured the blade of grass; a little green moisture seeped from the corner of her mouth. She licked the residue from nicotine-stained fingers. 'I don't suppose it's your fault, but I really have no time for your sort, I really don't.'

'Are you ready yet?' the girl called impatiently.

'Wait!' Swift was angry and angry at himself for expressing it towards the innocent child. 'What do you mean — my sort?'

'I lost my mother in Coventry. But I carry on. You have to carry on, don't you?'

'I see, so this is a hospital.'

'Oh well done. Well done.' The woman found a packet of cigarettes in the pocket of her blue apron.

'Then how did I get here?'

'Don't ask me. I'm just kitchen staff.'

'So you're not a nurse?'

'God, you're priceless you are. Bloody priceless.' She lit a cigarette and flicked her spent match towards the net. 'I could teach them . . . well, a thing or three. Twats.'

'When did you lose your mother?'

'Oh, you're a doctor now are you?'

'Clearly not, but . . .'

'Clearly not,' she mocked. 'So mind your own business.' The woman stood her ground; she seemed to have little inclination to return to the kitchens.

'All right,' Swift said stiffly. 'Yes, I will be coming in for dinner tonight. That's what you seemed to want to know so that's what I'm telling you.'

'Good for you. Good for you.'

'I'm serving now,' the girl called. 'Ready or not!'

The ball shied suddenly over the net, hitting the woman on the side of her head. It glanced off at an angle and went over the wall.

'You little bitch. You bitch!' The woman rubbed her head, she was fighting angry tears.

'Sorry,' the child called, unperturbed.

'I don't think there's any need for that, do you?' Swift said.

The woman looked at him with loathing and went back through the hole in the orange wall.

'Sorry,' the child called again. 'You serve.'

Swift picked up another ball and they locked back into synchronisation as the sun slowly dropped behind the far line of trees.

*

Later on he was sitting with a young doctor in a small room beside the ward. The window was open and Swift felt he could almost touch the cedar that dominated the square lawn beside the building. He was having difficulties with perspectives, something he was trying to explain to the man on whom he kept losing focus. The doctor had a face which settled easily into a mask of compassion; occasionally a remark of his would jolt it into interest, signalled by a brightening of the man's eyes, a lifting of his double chin, and an unfurrowing of his broad forehead. He was short, bald and overweight and wore a stethoscope round his neck rakishly like a stole.

'I suppose what I'm trying to talk about,' Swift said, 'is — I mean, the significance of things . . .'

'No, I don't know what you mean. Why don't you explain it to me?'

Swift shuffled on the canvas of his chair; his back

and legs were covered in bed sores. 'Well, what I mean is that everything has equal significance — even the most momentous occasions, but it's the course we choose to plot around these occasions which, only retrospectively, gives greater weight to one rather than the other.'

'So you don't believe in predetermination?'

'Of course not.'

'All right, give me an example.'

Swift felt both exhilarated and tired. 'I meet a woman on a train.'

'A stranger?'

'Yes. Yes. We talk for a while. I leave the compartment. I walk up the train. I ponder the conversation, the woman, I weigh the significance of the conversation and I return to the compartment having decided to score it highly. We get off the train together — our lives change. Does this make sense? Is this in any way new?'

'To you perhaps.'

'Oh.' Swift was immensely disappointed.

'The woman is killed in the blitz,' the doctor said, standing. 'It weighs heavily however you'd wish to see it.'

'Possibly,' Swift said.

'Of course.'

'But then significance is avoidable in all sorts of ways, isn't it? Insanity being but one refuge from it.'

'I have yet to meet a case of self-administered insanity,' said the doctor evenly.

'On the contrary, I would suggest the opposite to be the case.'

He could see the man composing his notes — delusion, he knew, would feature highly. But he was tired, so he excused himself and returned to the ward.

*

Later, after a brief nap, Swift continued his exploration of the hospital. He walked round the first-floor ward then found some back stairs which took him down to a brown corridor at ground level. The lino was worn in a wide central channel and the plaster on the walls was cracked. The tennis girl stood in a pool of light from one of the wide windows.

'They said you were a Cuthbert,' she said.

'A Cuthbert?'

'Somebody who doesn't want to fight.'

'Ah.'

'But I told them you weren't.'

'Good.'

'Will you play tennis?'

'Yes. But then I'm leaving.'

'Leaving?'

'Yes. I'm leaving the hospital.'

'All right.'

They followed the corridor round until they reached the boiler room and kitchen, stepping through the zebra stripes of light spilling through the wide windows. Swift felt as though he was watching an illusion, as though the wall was moving like a lit train flashing through an unlit station and he was standing still, watching it. They came to a door, the girl opened it and Swift followed her in. The room was dark, like a storeroom; he began to make out the broad shapes of the boilers, the air was hot and close, a pressure gauge loomed up at him like an eye. The door closed behind him and he waited like a blind man to be led forwards but the room was silent except for a faint electrical whine. He called, but nobody called back. He felt for the wall, found it, and sank to the floor.

THE VILLAGE

WHEN he awoke, Arnold was sitting cross-legged and flicking pebbles into the drying pond. A penumbra of mud surrounded the shallow water and the boy was aiming his missiles at its moist circumference. Swift swung his stiff legs from the bench.

'Oh, you're awake,' Arnold observed unenthusiastically. 'I've been waiting for ages.'

'You should have gone on.' Swift continued stretching as he joined Arnold by the pond. 'I told you to go on.'

'I know, sir.' Arnold looked up timidly. 'Only I didn't like to.' The boy began nibbling the bare flesh of his left knee, then he stopped and sniffed at the dampened area.

'Why not?' Swift lowered himself to his haunches.

'I didn't want to get lost. I thought if I got lost again there'd have been hell to pay.'

'Well, that's all right,' Swift said gently. 'I'm here now. And I won't let us get lost.'

'I think . . .' the boy began.

'Yes?'

'I'm afraid, sir.'

'Don't be silly. Come on.' Swift stood and the boy trailed two steps behind as they walked back to the lane. 'What are you afraid of?'

'I don't know.' The boy fell silent and Swift's attempts to draw him back into conversation were met with little enthusiasm. Despite Swift slowing almost to a stop, Arnold locked himself into step two yards behind, keeping his eyes fixed on his feet and the clouds of dust huffed by the friction of his soles against the road. Finally Swift could bear it no longer and rounded on the boy angrily for an explanation. 'What on earth is the matter!'

'It's nothing,' Arnold stammered.

'Well why are you so damned miserable?'

'I'm not miserable, sir. I'm hungry. And I've lost my gas mask.'

'Ah.' Swift softened his tone, but he was unpractised at showing concern and he auditioned a number of expressions until he found one he imagined would convey something in the way of warmth to the frightened boy. 'I can't do anything about your gas mask. But I can at least find some food.'

'Can you, sir?' Arnold's eyes interrogated him. 'Where?'

'You'll see. You'll see.' Swift held out his hand, the boy took it and they continued down the lane.

Swift didn't know how long he had slept, but he gauged it to have been no more than an hour. Even so, dusk had already begun to soften the line of the distant trees and it felt much later than it should have done. It was almost as if the day had surrendered an hour or so to the night, and while he had for the most part maintained his enthusiasm during the daylight hours, Swift didn't entirely welcome the coming darkness. The countryside unsettled him in a way no town ever did and he sensed the boy felt it too.

'Shall we play a game?' Swift said in an attempt to lighten both their moods.

'If you like.' The boy managed a little enthusiasm.

'Ahm. All right. I'll start. I spy with my little eye . . .' He paused and scanned the limited offerings in the lane: the vergeless track, dense hedges at either side, an approaching copse of tall trees and a few ragged shrubs sprouting from the foot of the bramble. It was a profoundly depressing landscape and it offered them no choices beyond going on or going back. '. . . Something beginning with T.'

'Trees!'

'No.'

'Yes it is.'

'No. Not trees . . . try again. Something beginning with . . .' He was talking as much for his benefit as the boy's. A twist of the lane had taken them among the trees; the track they were following losing definition. Swift pressed on but he was increasingly unsure whether he was taking them in the right direction. He heard a twig crack like a gunshot in the thick bushes to their right.

'Toad, sir.'

'What?'

'Toad. T for toad,' the boy said unconvincingly.

'Oh. Yes. Toad. That's right. Well done. Your turn.'

'You do know where we're going don't you, sir?'

'Of course I do. Don't worry.' Swift grasped the boy's hand tighter for reassurance. He saw with relief that there was a break in the trees ahead and steered the boy towards the window of light, even though it meant stepping among the thick roots of the surrounding trees which lay over the ground like amputated limbs. Something scurried across their path, tunnelling beneath the peaty carpet, and Arnold stopped dead.

'What was it!'

'I don't know,' Swift said. 'A vole, or a . . . hedge-hog.' His ignorance alarmed him. 'Please come on.' At least in the city the dangers were predictable. Who knew, Swift wondered, what they were going to confront next. They walked on in silence, then Arnold joined the game: 'I spy with my little eye . . .'

'Oh this is hopeless!' Swift released the boy's hand and looked unsurely ahead, then behind him.

'What, sir?'

'The . . . the . . . Oh just shut up a minute and let me think.'

For a second Swift had taken his eyes from the break in the trees and now he'd lost sight of it alto-gether. He was afraid that if they didn't find a way out of the wood soon, they'd have to remain there for the night, and the prospect of having to sleep on a bed of leaves with only the boy for company was not one he welcomed. He turned a slow circle to try and get a fix on where they were. Arnold was stand-ing stock still: a small bedraggled figure in a fully buttoned blazer with his cap pulled down low over his eyes. He no longer looked afraid, just resigned to never eating a square meal again.

'I spy with my little eye,' Arnold began again.

'Oh for God's sake!'

'Something beginning with L.'

'Arnold will you please . . .'

'Do you give up, sir?'

'Yes. Yes, I give up.'

'Light, sir.'

'Where?'

'There.' Arnold pointed through the gloom. Darkness, having established itself above the canopy of trees, now seemed to be rising from the floor of the wood, and with it a thin mist corrupting the last traces of warmth from the damp air.

'I should think it's a woodcutter's hut, sir. Perhaps we'll be welcomed by a good hearty meal.' Arnold set off towards the fairy tale promise of the light; Swift faltered then followed his lead. 'See. It is a hut,' Arnold said as they drew closer. A lamp burnt in the window but Swift could not differentiate any further detail; the setting was strangely reminiscent of somewhere he seemed to know quite well.

Arnold stopped by the door and left it to Swift to knock. 'Why put a lamp in a window?' Swift pondered.

'Perhaps he knew we were coming. Perhaps it's to help people like us who've lost their way. Shall you knock?'

Swift knocked and waited. Then he knocked again and pushed the door open. Arnold watched with a rare show of admiration, waiting for him to go in. Swift took a deep breath and stepped in; the boy held on to his sleeve. Inside it was almost bare; there was a wooden table, a bench and an incongruous black metal bedstead at an eccentric angle to the wall. Somebody was asleep beneath a grey blanket.

Swift pointed to the figure but Arnold had already seen it and was trying to get a closer look by standing on tiptoe and craning forwards like a tortoise extending its telescoped neck from its shell. Swift wasted a second wondering why the boy did not simply approach the bed, but it seemed he had reached an imaginary territorial limit and was unwilling to encroach further.

Swift stepped forwards, the floor creaked and the figure sat bolt upright.

'Oh it's you,' Swift said casually.

Arnold bounded forward and jumped onto the bed. The woman took off his cap, licked her finger and removed a smudge of mud from his cheek. The boy drew closer so that she was forced to put her arm round him. Arnold drew his knees to his chest and began sucking his thumb. Swift envied the boy his unconscious display of need. He wanted to be there, nestling close to the warmth of the woman.

'Come on. There's room for us all.' The woman patted the bed beside her.

'Why did you leave us?' Arnold challenged, lifting his head from the bed.

'I thought I'd go on while you played by the river. Then I got lost. It's quite easy to do, isn't it?'

'So it would seem,' Swift said heavily as he sat beside the woman on the bed, then lay back keeping as much distance between them as he could.

'I'm starving.' Arnold threw the accusation towards Swift then immediately fell asleep. The woman stroked the bristly hair on his neck; the boy shuddered and drew closer to her.

'And how are you?' the woman whispered to Swift.

'Oh marvellous. Absolutely marvellous,' he said bitterly.

'Your temper hasn't improved then.'

'I'd be a damned sight happier if I knew where we were.'

'I'm sure the village can't be far away.'

'But in which direction? Mm?'

The woman shrugged. Swift felt himself beginning to lean towards the hollow at the centre of the mattress. He transferred his energy towards tensing his elbows so that he didn't roll any further, then lay rigid to maintain his position. The woman watched his manoeuvres with curiosity.

'Doesn't it strike you as odd that we both stumbled on this place independently? And that it was open. And that there was a bed . . .?'

'Odd? Not particularly.' Swift was only half listening. His shift in concentration had taken him back to the brown suburban church where he was waiting for the coffin to arrive like a groom waiting for his bride. A boy had been found to play the organ. He was attacking the keyboard with gusto, experimenting with the stops and transposing the solemn march to a cheerful fairground burlesque. Swift could just see the round football of his head and plug ears bobbing up and down enthusiastically behind the choir stall as his short legs bounced on the pedals. The vicar appeared from the vestry then disappeared into another door pulling on his robes; the corner of a ham sandwich protruded like a tongue from his thick beard. The music stopped abruptly and, as the echo died, Swift heard a slap. The boy's head bobbed once more then he began rubbing his reddening ear vigorously. The music began again, solemnity restored, and the vicar appeared from behind a column smiling insincerely. He gathered his sleeves, forced the remainder of his sandwich into his mouth and pressed his thick white hands together.

Light lanced down the church as the heavy doors opened at the end of the aisle. Swift turned to see the coffin being brought in. It was carried by three men, vagrants they looked like, who had been pressed into ill-fitting suits with the promise of the price of a gin. None had shaved and the absence of a fourth shoulder meant that the front man had to walk backwards, supporting the coffin at shoulder height like an acrobat at the foot of a human pyramid. They arrived at the wooden trestles and staggered to a stop. The coffin was clattered down and the men sauntered back, talking loudly, up the aisle. Swift was left alone with the vicar and the boy as he waited for the service to begin.

'Doesn't it?'

Swift was aware of the woman again. 'Doesn't it what?'

'Doesn't it seem odd that we both . . .'

'Yes, found our way here. I know what you said, but I was thinking about . . .' He exhaled heavily. 'Oh, I don't know what I was thinking about.'

'What?' The woman prompted him gently.

'I was thinking about a funeral if you must know.'

'Whose — yours?'

'Don't be ridiculous.'

'Well whose?'

'My wife's as a matter of fact.'

'Tell me about her.' She rolled onto her side to face him with her curiosity so that their faces were no more than a foot apart. Swift looked into her eyes and knew that he wanted her: to release her soft whiteness from the constraining clothes: to see how her breasts would mound against each other, how the flesh of her thighs and stomach would give to his touch. He traced the line of her dry lips with his forefinger, but she took his hand away and guided it back to lie flat against his chest. 'Don't spoil it.'

'My wife?' he picked up smoothly. 'Yes, well I would hardly know where to . . . begin.'

'Where did you meet?'

'It was,' Swift smiled as he recalled the memory,

'. . . we met first on the top deck of a bus. Actually, I say we met, it was hardly a . . . I saw her. I saw her coming up the stairs because I was sitting on the back seat and I remember . . . first her hair: fair, straight, she had a fringe which hid her eyebrows and made her look a little severe, but her eyes — dark wonderful eyes: amused I would say and a slender nose and then a rather remarkable mouth: full lips, and I had this urge to kiss them there and then. And when she reached the top of the stairs she asked if the seat next to me was taken. It was really just a polite way of asking me to remove my briefcase which I did . . . and then we said no more. And she got off at Selfridges on Oxford Street. Yes, I watched her go back downstairs and I remember thinking that . . . she smiled as if to say she would really not have minded if I'd asked to see her again. In fact . . . in fact I got up to follow her, but the bus pulled away. And that was the first time. Yes.'

The church encroached again despite the woman's childish insistence that he tell her more. The music swelled through the tall space, the higher registers released by the boy's right hand soared to the rafters to chip like chisels at the thin silence. The bellowed bass rumbled weighty as waves through the cold air among the prayer cushions at his feet. The doors opened and Swift craned his neck to look again up the aisle.

'And then you married?'

'Married. Yes, we married within . . . within two

years of that first meeting. I was working in a bank just off Cavendish Square and I happened to see . . .'

'A bank?'

'Yes, as I said, I was working then in a . . .'

'So you were a manager?'

'No, not then, I was at the counter. Shall I go on?'

'Yes, please go on.'

'I was . . . I've lost my thread now . . .'

'You were at the counter.'

'Yes. And we met. And we married. And that was that. And then . . .' Swift looked down at Arnold's sleeping shape and knowledge arrived like the shock of a forgotten appointment.

'What is it?' the woman said, seeing something on his face.

At the same moment Arnold sat bolt upright. 'He would have swum but he said he was a little old for it,' the boy said, then sank down again, still asleep.

'I have a son,' Swift said.

Two

SWIFT heard someone calling. They were not calling him by name but he knew it was he that was being called. The voice was low and resonant, but unused to being raised so that the repeated 'hello' was tentative. Swift knew it could only be Patrick, despatched by his concerned sister to find him. He felt blindly for the door of the dark carriage and found it by groping his way along a row of wooden rake handles ranked in even intervals against the wall. He opened the door and saw Patrick immediately, standing in scarecrow silhouette at the edge of the allotment and peering intently in the wrong direction, his body bent forwards at the waist, his hands secured in his pockets. Swift felt a little sorry for him; even alone and unaware he was being observed, he was conscious enough of the image he was presenting to be embarrassed to have nothing with which to occupy his hands. Swift called and Patrick picked his way over the moonlit mounds and gulleys of earth towards him.

'You needn't have come,' Swift chided gently. 'I told Dorothy it would be all right.'

'I know you did.' Patrick shrugged with the merest gesture towards disloyalty.

Swift felt no such compunction. 'She bloody fusses too much. She always did.'

Patrick looked shamefaced, needlessly bearing a portion of the blame for the flaw in his wife's character. Swift relented. 'I'm sorry you had to come out. I should have come back sooner. What time is it?'

'A half past three.'

'Good God. And you've been up waiting for me?'

'Dorothy has. I'm afraid ten o'clock is all I can usually manage. Then it's off up the wooden road to Bedfordshire.' Patrick looked towards the segment of moon, bright and incongruous like a blade through a velvet curtain. The flannel collar of his pyjama jacket protruded above his cardigan. 'Beautiful night though, isn't it?'

'Yes.'

Patrick digested the moment in one bite, then said, 'Shall we go back?' He led off. 'Look, I'm sure Dorothy has said — well, I mean I'm sure she's spoken for us both, but really, please, if there's anything I can do that you feel she . . . well, I mean, she being your sister I imagine there's probably very little . . . nevertheless you know where I am, don't you. Telephone me at the office.' He stopped and Swift thanked him for what he assumed to have been an offer of sympathy. But it had not struck Swift when he woke that there was anything peculiar in waking in a railway carriage and when he had heard Patrick's voice the associations went only so far as Dorothy and the boys, stopping short of the night of the raid and the reason he was there. Patrick's halting offer brought it all flooding back.

'I'm afraid you rather upset Tom,' Patrick said.

'Did I? How?'

'He said you thought he was Arnold. Last night. I'm sure you didn't intend to but we try and shield the boys from . . . It's Dorothy you see.'

'Wait a minute.' Swift took Patrick's arm and forced him to stop. 'What are you trying to say?'

'I'm saying that the boys, Tom especially, are at rather an impressionable age and I would ask that . . .'

'Good God, she really does take the biscuit, doesn't she?'

'She has the boys' interests at heart. As indeed do I. That's all,' Patrick said stiffly.

'And does she imagine that I set out to alarm the boy? Good God, I mistook him for somebody else. It's quite typical of Dorothy to turn a simple case of mistaken identity into a crisis.'

'I hope you don't expect me to agree with that.' Patrick had toughened his tone, the point had been stretched too far even for him, but Swift pressed on indignantly. 'Of course not. Far be it from me to imagine you capable of independent thought.' He strode off, intending to leave Patrick stranded in the allotment, but the ground was uneven and after three long strides he found himself face down on the ground. He tasted earth and blood on his tongue. Patrick allowed him to scramble to his feet and brush himself down before coming over.

'I always forget,' Swift said soberly, 'how incompatible we are. Perhaps I find it hard to believe that not everyone feels the same about her.'

Patrick chose not to comment on Swift's observation. He had delivered Dorothy's message and now all he wanted to do was to go back to bed. He began walking away hoping that Swift would follow, but Swift was still perplexed by his nephew's reaction. He had always imagined Tom to be the less excitable of the two boys. It seemed to him unlikely that confusing him with another boy would have provoked any response let alone histrionics. And that led him to consider that perhaps the alarm lay in the name that he had used.

'Arnold,' Swift said out loud. The word was familiar, like the taste of milk stout on his palate. Patrick stopped. 'Arnold,' Swift said again. For an indefinable reason he felt his cheeks moisten and his breath catch in his throat. Patrick retraced his steps, took his hands from his pockets and laid them on Swift's arm. 'We didn't know,' he said gently. 'We didn't know what had happened to Arnold.'

THE HOSPITAL

A DOOR opened and the tennis girl stood in the rectangle of light from the garden. As Swift's eyes readjusted to the brightness in the boiler room he could see the damp orange wall of the tennis court behind her and the cedar tree protruding above it.

'Were you scared?' the child challenged.

'Yes. I was a little.'

'I didn't do it on purpose, I don't know where the light is.' She twisted like a dancer on the spot and ran off into the garden. Swift walked carefully round the boilers, skirting the deep drop around each of the large black cylinders. Then he climbed two stone steps using the metal handrail for support and found himself in the kitchen garden. The girl was waiting for him, already thirty yards away, standing in the gap in the orange brick wall.

'Must you leave?' she called to him.

'I have to find my son,' Swift called back.

'You didn't say you had any children.' The child stalked jealously through the hole in the wall, Swift followed and found her sitting on the grass court facing towards the house. He sat behind her and waited.

Finally she said, 'I thought we weren't going to have any secrets.'

'It wasn't a secret.'

'Then why didn't you tell me?'

'I don't think I knew myself.'

The girl shuffled to face him, unsure whether or not she was being teased. 'Is that why you're here?'

'I think it may be. One of the reasons anyway.'

'Of course it is. Don't make it any more complicated than it has to be.'

Swift laughed. 'I'm not trying to make it complicated. I'm just trying to unravel the puzzle.'

The child leapt to her feet as a charge of energy hit her. 'You don't unravel a puzzle. You unravel a ball of string. A puzzle is made to be complicated, a ball of string gets tangled by mistake.'

'No, I still maintain you can unravel a puzzle.'

'And besides, a ball of string has only one end to find and it gets tangled in itself, but a puzzle may have all sorts of riddles to solve. Don't you want to play tennis?'

'Of course I do. I'm not the one who is...'

'Here then.' She curtseyed and picked up the two racquets from the light green silhouettes they had left in the long grass. 'The thing with string, though, is that people only unravel enough for themselves and leave the rest in a mess. I think you should untangle the whole ball. I'll serve.'

Before Swift could position himself to receive, the girl served a swerving ball hard over the net. It bounced into a flower bed. 'Fifteen love.'

'I thought we were going to knock up first,' Swift said. 'You know. To beat the record.'

'No. That's child's play. Play!' Another ball shied over the net, Swift barely saw it as it came out of the sun and sped past him.

'Thirty love.'

'I wasn't ready for that!'

'I've decided I've been too kind to you. It's time for a proper game.'

'Wait.' Swift held up his hand, the girl relaxed her stance but maintained the pressure on him with the fierceness of her expression. 'Look, let's get this sorted out, can we?'

'I thought we were playing tennis,' the girl said.

'We are. We are.' Swift approached the net. 'I don't want you to think that I've misled you. That's all.'

'Oh, I don't think you did. Not on purpose anyway.' A blush of anger remained on her cheek. 'I don't want to talk. I just want to play. There's too much talking here, it's too serious.'

To the child's annoyance Swift remained at the net. 'Then why are you here?'

'Because my mother is here.' Something caught

her eye, she transferred her attention towards a high window in the eaves of the house.

'Is she working here?'

'No, she's just here.'

'Visiting then?'

'She's always shouting at people. I think they're waiting for her to stop shouting.'

'I'm sorry.' The truth cemented the bond between them. 'But what about your father — can't he help?'

'No. He's no use. He's abroad.'

'I see. He's fighting is he?'

'I imagine he is.' She laid the racquet down and walked solemnly away towards an uncharted part of the garden. Swift wanted to call her back but recognised the impotence of the gesture. He had nothing to offer her in the way of hope or solace. The child was scouting towards the line of trees that fringed the formal part of the garden. Above them Swift could see a procession of smoke rising in percussive bursts from a slow-moving train. The smoke caught the girl's attention and seemed to shake her from her mood. Her slow introverted saunter became a hop, then a skip, then a dash towards the trees. Swift set off after her; he was invigorated by her vigour and although he could not match her pace the movement loosened the last stiffness from his legs. His lungs were leaden but he felt free. He knew now that he had a son, and the remembering of it gave him a reason to live.

THE VILLAGE

B Y the morning, the dampness from the wood had permeated the hut. The small windows were misted with condensation. Swift lay on the bed and vented his breath from the funnel of his mouth into the cold air. Hunger had turned from an ache to a pain; he flexed his stomach muscles and they responded tautly behind the notched-in belt of his trousers. He was cold and uncomfortable; a layer of moisture had formed inside his vest; he became aware of it when he rolled over onto his side and found the woman awake on the bed, watching him.

'You look much younger when you think there's nobody looking at you; when you don't have to put on an act.'

'And good morning to you,' he said, sitting up stiffly.

'I think that rather proves my point, doesn't it?' The woman was lying on her stomach, resting her chin on her tented fingers as if she was sunning her back. 'And by the way, Arnold's gone.'

'Has he?' Swift said without interest, going to the

window. The lamp had burnt out; he moved it aside and wiped a pane clear of soot and condensation.

'I thought you'd be concerned.' She rolled onto her back, then sat up; her bare feet felt for her shoes on the floor.

'I'm not concerned. He can do what he damned well likes. I'm not responsible for him.'

'Aren't you? I thought you were. I thought you'd decided to be responsible for us all.'

'Absolutely not,' he echoed. 'He can do what he damned well likes.'

Through the window Swift watched as the long fingers of early sun reached through the flaws in the forest cover. The undergrowth steamed as it warmed. Swift went to the door and stretched. The silence unnerved him, and as he stepped from the hut he felt as though he was being observed by a thousand pairs of eyes. In the distance a shrill whistle cut through the silence. He listened for a repeat but none came. The woman followed him out.

'Is the war still going on, or has it finished do you think?' she said.

'It has finished. And when we return to the city it will re-start. They will stage-manage it for us.' An image sprang to his mind of a gutted cathedral, like the upturned hull of a ship, beached, bleached and stripped to its ribs by the sea.

'So people have stopped dying?' She looked at him with hope.

'Oh yes, and if we remain here then there will be no more deaths.'

'Then we shall stay.'

'I'm not sure whether I could bear that,' Swift said.

The woman linked her arm in his and laid her head against his arm. 'I think we need to find Arnold.'

'Do we? Why?'

'I just think we do. I think we should stay together, otherwise we might all be lost.'

'And then we can go back for the train.'

'Yes. I suppose we can.'

Swift allowed himself to be led towards the wall of trees fringing the small clearing. He resigned himself to the inevitability of fate, feeling that he had long since lost any influence over his destiny. He knew he was expected in Manchester, but when, and by whom, seemed to have become increasingly unimportant. He knew he had wanted to flee there after the raid; to be absorbed into the home of Patrick and Dorothy, who would care for him and temporarily relieve him of the arduous burdens of choice. But now it seemed that the woman was fulfilling his sister's role, and the more he allowed her to take on the less he felt inclined to get to Manchester.

'You were telling me about your wife,' the woman said.

'Yes, I was, wasn't I. But I don't think I want to

talk about her any more. To be quite honest I don't see that it's any of your business.'

'I see.' The woman tugged her arm away.

'I'm sure you don't.' The past was a burden he could not relinquish, but he could carry it so long as he was not forced to confront it.

'You're so dry, Mr Bowler. Like a stiff dishcloth. Stick your head under a tap: refresh yourself back to life.'

'Oh, I'm quite alive; in any case, as alive as I'd ever wish to be.'

'Then share it!' She pushed him playfully in the ribs, then darted out of his reach, inviting him to do the same to her.

'I have no need to share it,' Swift said sullenly. 'I'm quite self-sufficient.'

'No, you can't be. You can't give up. I won't let you.'

'I'm afraid it's out of my control.'

They had reached the edge of the clearing. Swift felt disinclined to go further into the wood; he had lost all sense of direction.

'Listen.' The woman took his hand. 'You said you were afraid to live. Remember?' Swift nodded. He had a strong urge to cry without knowing why. 'And you blamed the war, and I said . . .'

'I know what you said.'

'So this self-sufficiency is not born of choice at all, but out of fear.'

'I'm sure I haven't the faintest idea of what you're talking about.'

'Well I think you're just like the rest of us and it's not life you fear at all but death. And so you choose to live your life in suspended animation so that when the moment actually arrives you imagine there will be little difference from the way you conduct your life now.'

'Thank you for the character analysis.' An image flicked past the corner of his eye of a figure hurrying into a room.

'So you don't think it's true?'

'Not in the least.' A ball bounced at his feet.

'Arnold!' he called.

'Forty love,' a child called back. 'Game point.'

'Arnold!' he called again, feeling suddenly feverish as though the heat of the new day had tangled round him like damp sheets.

'Gregory, it's all right.' A cool hand went to his forehead. He opened his eyes and saw his sister holding her pink flannel dressing-gown closed with a tight fist and her pained, tired face creased with concern.

'I really had the most awful . . .' He turned to face the wall of the small guest bedroom, forcing her to break the contact.

'I think you should see a doctor.'

It seemed still to be night. The house was silent, the curtains drawn, but a light burnt behind Swift's eyes that went beyond tiredness and towards revelation. He forced his concentration towards the tiny red flowers on the mustard patterned wallpaper and found that by clenching his eyes half shut he could animate them into flames.

'I said I think you should see a doctor,' Dorothy said again.

'I'm sorry,' Swift said. 'Am I becoming an inconvenience?'

'Don't be ridiculous.' Dorothy compensated for his suggestion by injecting a note of false levity into her voice which made it sound more brittle and alarmed. Swift did not roll over. He had no need to, he knew exactly which of his sister's masks of disapprobation she would be wearing. It would be the one she reserved for the old and the infirm; he had seen it used to effect on their mother when she had asked for a bedpan in the last sleepless week before her death: an expression that suggested her infirmity was nothing compared to the inconvenience it was causing. But with that came the guilt, which was entirely his. It was his sister and not he, after all, who had been caring for her.

'Do you want to talk about it?' Having made the uncomfortable offer, Dorothy sat on the bed even though talking about it was the very last thing she wanted to do and the offer seemed to have surprised her no more than it surprised him.

'Talk about it?' Swift sat up.

'Yes. Patrick said . . . well, no matter what he said.

The important thing is what we are going to do with you.'

'You're not going to do anything with me, Dorothy. Not without my permission, anyhow.'

Dorothy tried to read his face before replying. She had made a conscious choice not to be angry, instead she tried to soothe him. 'You know I wouldn't do that, Gregory.'

Tom appeared briefly like a ghost in the doorway then passed on, switching off the corridor light.

'What time is it?' Swift felt as though he had been asleep for hours. His head sang with energy.

'It's a quarter to five. Was that Patrick?' She had turned as the light clicked off; Swift was fascinated by the glimpse of her hair nested tightly in a net. When she turned back he could see a little more of their mother in her eyes: inquisitive, amused, though Dorothy had always worn her life with much less ease.

'I always felt guilty about them you know,' Swift confided.

'What?'

'Mother and father.'

'Oh, yes, well. I expect you have every reason to,' she said sharply, unable to keep the pact she had made with herself.

'No. It was nothing to do with the end of it. I wasn't thinking of that at all. It was way before that really . . . from when, I don't know, I suppose when I left home.'

'Well,' Dorothy replied matter of factly, 'I think there's little point in pursuing that now, is there?'

'Why?'

'Because . . . because it's the middle of the night. And there's a time and a place for everything.' She was already occupied with the practicalities of the day and wondering whether it was too early to call out the doctor. But she had been deeply disturbed by Swift's cries in the night and his eyes remained startled and opaque.

'I'm afraid I have to disagree. I think there is neither a time nor a place for anything unless you make one. And I should very much like to talk about them now.'

His mood had swung so that now he seemed to be on the verge of tears and Dorothy gave way to his indignant outburst.

'I was thinking about grandmother just then. Her dark room. Small, dark front room. With the silver teapot . . . the dead fire in the grate, but the smell of it still there. Do you remember?' He watched, wanting to take Dorothy with him: back through it all. 'The brass-handled brush by the grate and scuttle and the carpet smell of . . . childhood. Mm? And we used to play under the table when we were small and make the most marvellous dens and sit among their legs and they didn't mind, and Father would pass us sandwiches down and we'd share a plate. Then we'd argue, but it didn't seem to matter. And we'd scrap and then we'd catch the train and fall asleep on their laps and it would be dark when we got back to the town and they'd wake us and Mother would dress us in our pyjamas while Father made up a fire and he'd read us a story together. Both of us together in his lap on Sunday nights. Remember? Then we'd go up to bed and sometimes Mother would play the piano and you could just hear it through the floor.'

'Yes I remember.'

'Like that? Do you remember it like that?'

'Yes.'

'You see I almost wonder if there is any difference between being there and simply remembering. I almost wonder if there is.' Swift startled Dorothy from the bed with a flurry of activity which left her standing beside the door. 'I think I'd better leave.' He had a mission, revealed to him in the selective memories of his childhood, and his mission, he now knew, was to find his son.

'Gregory, it's the middle of the night,' Dorothy said, alarmed at the prospect of him wandering the streets in his present condition.

'No matter. I'll get the milk train.' He removed his pyjama trousers and stood naked from the waist down while he scouted round for his clothes.

'Gregory please!' The ludicrousness of the spectacle almost caused her to laugh out loud, but she held it back. 'You're being quite ridiculous.'

'Where are my clothes?'

'They're in the linen basket.'

'Then get them out.'

'You'll have to borrow some of Patrick's.' Dorothy averted her eyes as she left the room. Swift sat on the bed and Tom reappeared at the door, unable to sleep because of the commotion.

'Hello,' Swift said to the staring boy.

'You don't have to go, you know.'

'I know, but I need to go.'

'Where?'

'Back to London. I have to find Arnold.'

'But I thought you said,' his forehead furrowed, 'I thought you said he was dead.'

'Oh I see!' Swift laughed joyously and the boy's confusion grew; adults did not behave like this in his parents' house. He had once, however, seen a man shouting at a lamp-post, and his mother had told him that the man was a lunatic. There was something of the look in that man's eye on the face of his favourite uncle and it frightened him. But Swift had laughed merely because he now understood Patrick's earlier admonishment. 'I'm sorry, Tom. I'm sorry. I'm not laughing at you.'

'So Arnold is alive?' the boy tried, tentatively.

'Yes. Yes. Yes, of course he is, he's ... he's at school. Yes, he's at school.'

'Good.' The boy drifted away, bleary eyed. He had never really enjoyed Arnold's company and found it hard to associate the rather melancholic child with the warmth he always felt in the company of his uncle. But the idea of him having perished had been too enormous to accept. The war, as far as he was concerned, was being conducted as a series of chess moves on a *War Weekly* map, it was a scavenging for hot shards of metal in bombed-out buildings, silhouettes of fighter aircraft on his bedroom wall. Even the roll call of 'old boys who have fallen' at assembly was more thrilling than tragic. He now felt that his refusal to accept Arnold's death may have had some bearing on his resurrection and he made a mental note to mention it to him when next they met.

Swift heard a whispered conversation in the hall-way and Patrick came in, clearly having just woken.

'It's, ah . . .' He consulted his watch. 'Yes. Nearly five o'clock.' He announced the time as he would have done in response to having been asked to give it.

'I know. I'm sorry, Patrick, but I'm leaving.'

'Fine.' He struggled to shake off his tiredness as he edged into the room, then saw Swift's state of undress and came in no further. 'Fine.'

'I have to find Arnold, you see,' Swift said, feeling Patrick deserved the same explanation as Tom.

'Yes. Yes, I'm sure you do. Tom tells me . . . well, that Arnold is still at school. Is that right?'

'Oh yes. I'm going there now. To get this all sorted out.'

'Yes, but you see, I was led to believe . . . that, well, that he had perished too.'

'Yes, so I understand.'

'I'm sorry.' Patrick felt defeated and confused. 'I'm sorry, I really don't understand at all.' Dorothy arrived with an armful of Patrick's underwear. 'If he is, as you say, alive. And I'm so glad to hear it. I wonder why you didn't go straight to him. Or did you telegraph him about his mother's death?'

Before Swift could answer, or even formulate an answer in his mind, Dorothy cut in, 'I'm lending Gregory a few things. You don't mind, do you?' She deposited them on the bed beside him and Swift lifted the top pair of underpants, looked at them, then tried them for size. Dorothy and Patrick watched him, she intently to see whether they fitted, and he bound by a set of conventions which somehow made it harder for him to leave than to remain.

'How are they?' Dorothy said.

'Comfortable. Very comfortable.' Swift flexed his right leg, enjoying the support.

'You can borrow the others. I'll fetch you a bag.' Dorothy again scuttled out of the room, sublimating her unmanageable concern for his welfare beneath a practical concern for his warmth. This time her leaving left a vacuum in the room and when Swift looked up he saw that Patrick was staring at him blankly in a manner similar to Tom's a few minutes before. 'This isn't some sort of . . . joke, is it?'

'Of course it's not a joke.'

'I hope not. I do hope not.' Patrick had clearly reached, and been pushed beyond, the limits of his known world. He had always harboured a suspicion that Swift looked down on him, perhaps even secretly despising him for marrying Dorothy. The suspicion resurfaced whenever they spent more than a short time together and always vanished on Swift's departure.

Gregory Swift was the kind of man who was regarded by Patrick, and by those who didn't know him particularly well, as supercilious, but he would have been shocked to hear it. Like Dorothy, he found more foolishness than wisdom in the people he knew, but unlike his sister he had married someone with identical perceptions. Much of his sister's frustration lay in the fact that she had chosen to match herself with Patrick, who, unlike Gregory, could not see through her. So it was inevitable that it was towards Gregory that she directed much of her irritation.

'Don't worry, Patrick. Life will return to normal when I leave.' Swift forgave him the accusation.

'I'm sorry. Ludicrous thing to suggest... absolutely ludicrous. Look...' He came tentatively further into the room. 'Look...'

'Please!' Swift said, reading the signs on Patrick's face. 'No more sympathy. No more understanding. I've had quite as much of it as I can bear. And quite frankly after a certain amount it ceases to have any meaning whatsoever. So please, Patrick. No more.'

'No, I was merely going to ask whether you were short of cash. That's all.'

'Ah.' Swift smiled, defeated by his generosity. 'No. No I'm not, but thank you.'

Dorothy arrived with a small suitcase for his borrowed belongings, then she and Patrick left him alone to dress.

When he was ready he peered along the hallway and then walked carefully and silently down the stairs. As he reached the bottom he sensed he was being watched and when he turned round he saw Tom peering through the bannisters at him.

'Are you leaving now?' Tom whispered.

'Yes. Goodbye Tom.'

The boy crept down two steps and sat dangling his legs from the landing.

'Will you write?'

'Of course I will.' Swift blew a kiss to the confused child and let himself out of the house.

The first glimmerings of dawn were appearing over the allotment, bathing the trellises in a dull grey light. The sky hung like slate. Swift found it inconceivable that any growth was occurring beneath the surface of the ground and then realised that he was contemplating his wife sleeping alone in the inert earth. He shrugged off a cold shiver then set off towards the main road that would take him back into the city.

'I've found the way.' Arnold reappeared through a gap in the trees. 'I thought you'd never wake up so I went on on my own. There's a hotel and a shop.'

'Lead the way then.' The woman laughed and linked her arm in Swift's as they set off after the boy. He took them left through the densest cluster of trees then over a stile and through a field of sheep. Arnold tried vaulting the gate at the far end of the field but its height defeated him and he arrived untidily like a dropped sack of potatoes on the other side. Shamefaced, he dusted himself down as the two adults climbed carefully and adultly after him. He had grazed his knee but Swift chose not to draw attention to it on the grounds that the minimal physical discomfort the boy was experiencing was far outweighed by his hurt pride. The woman patted his head instead and the economical gesture of concern was sufficient to spur him on.

Shortly afterwards they reached the lane which broadened into the high street of the village. One side was lined with a no-nonsense collection of utilitarian shops with sawdusted steps dropping into dark interiors; on the other was a row of squat cottages of honey-coloured stone weathered to grey and terraced beneath steep slate roofs punctuated by one-pot chimneys. Beyond those, like a full stop beneath an exclamation mark, a small country hotel stood square-on, so that the road, on arriving at its swinging sign, forked and then, Swift presumed, rejoined behind it. A two-seater open-topped car was parked in front of the hotel but there was no other sign of habitation.

'I suppose it's still early.' The woman voiced Swift's concern that they had stumbled across a ghost town, while Arnold continued confidently leading the way towards the hotel, his cap still firmly in place, his blazer buttoned tight. Since his disappearance that morning, Swift had begun to take a dislike to the boy which he rationalised into a desire to be alone with the woman. He had greeted his return with scorn but the boy had disregarded him and instead directed his enthusiastic babble towards the woman. Only when he'd failed to clear the gate did Swift find a bond between them reestablished, misfortune striking a deeper note of paternalism in him than childish optimism.

'Come on you two, hurry up!' Arnold, having arrived first at the hotel, bowled gracelessly through the ivy curtain overhanging the porched doorway. Swift followed the boy into the timbered reception and caught sight of him disappearing through another door. His instinct was to wait for a member of staff to arrive but the woman had other ideas and followed Arnold into the dining-room.

There were six tables in the small brown shadowed room. Arnold had taken a seat by the grimy French windows which were lapped by an unkempt lawn. At another table beside the door an elderly man in a dressing-gown was intricately dissecting a boiled egg. Swift nodded a greeting.

'Oh there you are,' the man said. 'You're with the little fellow, are you?'

Swift went over and they shook hands, the man remaining seated as he introduced himself as Arthur Pettigrew. Swift explained the circumstances of their arrival but Pettigrew seemed uninterested so he returned to Arnold's table and opened the menu folder. The card inside had, however, been removed, so the three of them sat patiently waiting for somebody to come to serve them, Arnold enviously watching Arthur Pettigrew's fastidious destruction of his egg.

'Have you come far?' Pettigrew laid down his spoon.

'From London,' Swift said, confused, having less than two minutes before imparted to him the details of their journey.

'Yes? I came from London.'

'How long have you been here?' The woman

sensed that Pettigrew was interested in them solely as an audience.

'Oh . . . a year. Possibly two.' Pettigrew lifted the corner of a linen tea-towel draped over a small basket at the centre of the table and removed another egg, which he then inserted into the egg cup.

'You must like it here.'

'Yes, I suppose I must.'

'Do you think we might get some breakfast?' Swift, like Arnold, was now resenting Arthur Pettigrew's systematic breakfasting.

'I don't imagine you intended to come here?' Pettigrew addressed the question to the egg. Like many people who have for a protracted period lived alone, he now communicated solely within his own agenda.

Arthur Pettigrew's eyes were egg yellow, but the most striking aspect of his appearance was his thick eyebrows which were tethered to his forehead like two windblown bushes on an exposed hillside. His white cotton-wool hair ceased abruptly at the low waterline of his domed head and his sombre features were underlined by a thin mouth taut with self obsession.

'There is, however, a reason,' Pettigrew continued, 'even if that reason is not at this moment apparent.'

Swift and the woman exchanged glances. 'I wonder if you'd care to explain that remark?'

Arthur Pettigrew blotted a flake of yolk from his lip with a clumsy hand. 'There.' He rubbed his hands with the air of a job well done and carried his empty plate through the beaded curtain at the end of the room.

'Peculiar man.' Swift looked to the others for confirmation. 'I wonder what he meant.'

'I'm sorry?' The woman interrupted a silent conversation initiated by Arnold which involved mute expression and exaggerated hand signals.

'What he meant. I wonder what he meant.'

'Oh, I'm sure I haven't an idea.'

'Did I interrupt something?' Swift said.

'No.' The woman smiled at Arnold, 'We were just saying that Arthur Pettigrew looks like an egg himself.'

Arnold stifled a laugh which nevertheless escaped like a hoarse bark; tears of mirth sprang into his eyes.

'I don't think that sort of comment is very helpful. Do you?' Swift began tapping the table impatiently.

The room, although set for breakfast, had an air of disuse. A grandmother clock was frozen at ten minutes to four, cobwebs hung like frost on the curtains, the tables and floor were coated with a layer of damp dust which clung stickily to the waxed surfaces. Looking hopefully towards the beaded curtain for someone to take their order, Swift saw Arnold resume his telegraphed conversation with the woman.

'Oh for God's sake!' Swift pushed his chair back from the table and walked out of the room. He heard Arnold and the woman laugh behind him.

The bead-curtained room seemed to be an annexe of a larger kitchen. The stove and tables were stacked like a church bazaar with piles of unmatching crockery, the sink overflowing with filthy plates. He walked through to a larger stone-flagged floor and the temperature dropped. The second room was tiled but empty. Swift discerned its purpose to be a cold store although there were no carcasses suspended from the metal racks on the ceiling and the gulley which ran down the centre of the room to a drain was dry. A door at the far end of the room took him back to the reception desk where he found Arthur Pettigrew asleep in a winged chair, his bare feet caressing each other beside discarded leather slippers, his shins marble white beneath his pyjama trousers.

Swift struck the brass bell and the pure note rang out stridently causing Pettigrew to open his eyes. He moved no other muscle. 'I was rather hoping we could get some food.'

'I'm sorry, we're closed,' Pettigrew said without any trace of warmth and closed his eyes. Swift struck the bell again and again Pettigrew responded by opening his eyes, this time with a glint of anger showing in them.

'I wonder whether you could supply us with some breakfast. The boy hasn't eaten since yesterday.'

'I'm afraid that's your problem,' Pettigrew said. 'You can't hold me responsible for your lack of foresight.'

'I don't hold you responsible for anything,' Swift said, managing to hold on to his temper. 'All I wondered was whether it would be possible for us to eat.'

'As I think I have already explained, service here has been terminated. Thank you for your enquiry.'

'Surely . . . surely you wouldn't mind allowing us something. In the circumstances.'

Pettigrew sucked his teeth and lifted his cheek from the wing of the chair, the leather rasping as the moist contact was broken. 'I really don't know how else I can put it.' He furrowed his brow as though that was exactly what he was attempting to do.

'Then I shall remain here until you change your mind.' Swift flipped open the visitors' comments book. The padded leather cover hit the reception desk with a loud slap and a cloud of dust rose from the pages. Pettigrew eyed him warily as he began reading out the contents. 'Mr and Mrs Vincent of Matlock Bath were clearly impressed, indeed they even go to the trouble of commenting on the food. Let's see; Hattie Coyne found the weather inclement but the evening company delightful. I wonder if perhaps you were away that particular week?'

'There is no food,' Pettigrew reiterated.

'Then find some.' Swift had become immediately

engrossed by the comments in the book. None was more than five lines but all suggested a clear picture of who had written them. Hattie Coyne clearly travelled alone and had been entertained in the long tedious evenings by Mr and Mrs Vincent of Matlock Bath (he deduced this by the coinciding arrival and departure dates of the adjoining entries; Coyne and the Vincents had enjoyed three evenings in each other's company). The Vincents were on a motoring holiday and were keen to advertise the fact that they owned a car by commenting on the 'quaint and narrow roads' and, being childless (Swift decided), were seeking to compensate by travel. Hattie Coyne had caught the eye of Mr Vincent who dearly wanted to take her for a spin but was unwilling to broach the subject with his wife (a suspicious woman prone to neuralgia). Her suspicions were not without good reason, Mr Vincent having conducted at least one longstanding affair with a barmaid who worked in one of the hotels in Matlock Bath.

'Hattie Coyne,' Swift said, 'remember her?'

'There is nowhere I can get food.' The change in Pettigrew's tone from obstructiveness to defeat prompted Swift to shake himself from further contemplations of Hattie Coyne which had taken a decidedly carnal turn. 'My credit has run out — and now I survive on filched eggs. Are you satisfied?'

'Here.' Swift took out his wallet and laid a ten shilling note on the counter. 'I fully expected to pay.'

'I don't think you understand, do you?' Pettigrew began muttering to himself as he took the note and ambled out of the hotel. Swift watched him proceed down the centre of the street before turning into a shop.

'What a sad man.' The woman emerged from the dining-room.

'Were you listening?'

'All that sadness and nowhere to put it.'

'He's just a miserable old fool. I imagine he's made everyone's life such a misery that they've all deserted him. I mean could you work for someone like that?'

'You are in a charitable mood today, aren't you, Mr Bowler?'

'I wonder if he has a telephone.' Swift leant over the desk then poked his head into a small paper-cluttered office.

'What difference does it make?'

'My sister is expecting me — in Manchester. I thought I'd already explained all that.' The return to civilisation had re-inspired Swift towards the initial purpose of his visit.

'I see.'

'What do you mean "you see"?'

The woman sighed heavily. 'Nothing. Nothing at all.'

'Look. You might be quite content to wander around this bloody village for the rest of your life. I'm not. I have to get to Manchester.'

'Why?'

'Because it's been arranged. That's why.'

'I really don't see that a day can make all that difference.'

'Don't you?'

'Not in the present circumstances, no.'

'I'm sorry? I wasn't aware of a change in our circumstances.' Swift gave up his search and went to the door. 'I suppose there would be telegraph poles, wouldn't there — if the village was connected to the local exchange.'

'It's just that I can't bear to go on. Not yet.'

Swift allowed a minute to pass before taking up the comment. He was aware that, having done so, he would be unable to retract his interest and he was unsure he could shoulder any further burdens. 'It's been hard for you, I know, but you have to face up to . . .' His attempt to divert her resulted in the woman pushing angrily past him. 'Thank you for your concern, Mr Swift — and goodbye!'

'Look.' Swift caught her arm, frantically formulating a retraction. 'Look, I'm sorry.'

'I should think you are.'

'Please hear me out.'

'I don't want to hear you out.' She shook herself free of the contact. 'I want someone to hear me out. Do you understand!' The force of her anger took Swift aback; he found himself nodding mutely as Arnold arrived, drawn by the commotion. The boy spectated from the safety of the dining-room doorway.

'I said, do you understand!' The woman hammered her fist into Swift's chest.

'Yes. I'm sorry. Yes I do.'

'Then just listen.' She cast a cold look towards Arnold which he rightly interpreted as an invitation to leave but his hunger was now so acute that he welcomed any diversion from it, however unpleasant. 'Both of you then. Both of you . . .' She drew in a deep breath. 'I'm so tired. So, so tired of all the pain.' Swift nodded encouragement. She turned to Arnold, pleading now for the child's attention. 'I just . . . I just couldn't bear it. I had to leave.'

'That's perfectly understandable. Perfectly.' Swift turned to Arnold for confirmation. The boy stared back blankly; he was merely acting as a prism between them, refracting the sense of each statement; his silence breaking each sentence down to its constituent meanings.

'No it's not, you have no idea of what I'm saying; I sat with him you see. All night. He was just a boy . . . and they told me I shouldn't but I couldn't bear the thought of him being alone.'

'Who? Who did you sit with?' Swift's interest was genuine but selfish; it seemed to have a bearing on his own circumstances but exactly what was unclear.

'A boy. I don't know, just a boy.' Arnold walked to her like a ghost, his eyes never leaving her face;

she drew him towards her for comfort and laid her cheek on the sparse hair of his head. 'Arnold understands.'

'I understand,' Swift said. 'At least I think I do.'

'It doesn't matter.'

'You were sitting with a child in the hospital . . . and . . .'

'He was dead, wasn't he?' Arnold volunteered the solution to the riddle.

'Yes,' the woman whispered. 'It wasn't my fault.'

'I'm sure nobody was suggesting it was.' Swift's concern with the literal truth provoked a look of displeasure from Arnold. It seemed that again Swift had been excluded by the woman and the child even though now, more than at any other time, he wanted to understand.

'Do you know what I thought?' The woman released Arnold from the embrace. 'I thought . . .' She gestured vaguely with her hand.

'Please, go on,' Swift encouraged.

'I thought . . . I thought, as we were walking to the village, that we were all dead: the three of us; and somehow we were walking through this beautiful land towards . . . Do you have any faith, Mr Bowler?'

'Yes, I have faith.'

'That's what I believed: that we'd all . . . and we were walking through Heaven. Ridiculous, isn't it?' She laughed self-consciously; Swift was unsure whether it was a signal for him to join in. 'Ridiculous.' Her laughter ended abruptly.

'And how did we die?' Swift said.

'In the raid. It was the others who survived. Not us.'

'I don't think this is Heaven at all.' Arnold went to the door like a dog waiting to be walked. 'I think I should like to go back please.'

'I think you're right,' the woman concurred. 'I think we should leave here and go back to the station.'

From his narrow view of the street, Swift could see Pettigrew's slow, slippered return from the shop. 'Perhaps we should wait for breakfast.'

'No. I don't like it here.' The boy was clearly afraid.

'I thought you were hungry?'

'Yes, I am. But I should still like to go.'

The woman took Arnold's hand. 'I think he's right. I think we should go.'

'But what's the rush? I'm sorry but I just don't understand.' It was clear to Swift that the woman and the child were feeding each other's hysteria. It seemed that they had become so close that soon there would be no need for verbal communication whatsoever.

Without a word they left, hand in hand, passing Pettigrew in the street without acknowledging him, and setting off in the direction of the station. Swift waited, feeling that the man deserved an explanation before they all deserted him.

'I have a room for you all.' Pettigrew walked in and deposited a loaf of bread on the counter before brushing the flour from his dry hands.

'Yes, I'm sorry to have put you to any trouble but we're leaving.'

'But I have a room for you all.'

'Yes, but we're going for the train now. We won't be requiring breakfast.'

'Yes.' Pettigrew grasped the post at the foot of the bannisters. 'Perhaps you'd at least have the good grace to look at it.' He started up the stairs and Swift felt that he had no choice but to follow him. At the top, they walked along a short unlit corridor to the end door. Pettigrew pushed it open and Swift walked in.

The room was musty and damp; green mould was spreading over the whitewashed walls; the ceiling was bowed and cracked, the stained single mattress unmade.

'I'm sorry, I don't understand . . .'

'I could let you have it at reduced rates.'

'No, you see, we're not staying.'

'Oh.' Pettigrew seemed genuinely confused. 'You don't want the room then?'

'I have to get to Manchester.' Swift bent down to look through the cracked panes of the low window. He could just see Arnold and the woman turning the bend at the top of the high street. The floor-boards were spongy with rot.

'Then you won't be requiring a room.' Pettigrew leant in and ushered Swift out, closing the door behind him. 'I thought, you see, that you might stay for a few days.' In the virtual darkness of the narrow corridor, Swift's exit was blocked and he was suddenly afraid of the old man despite knowing he could easily overpower him.

'Will you let me pass?' Swift pushed gently into Pettigrew but he had wedged himself in the corridor, his back against one wall, his toes against the other.

'I could show you the Vincents' room. From Matlock Bath. Perhaps you would prefer to stay in there?'

'I really wouldn't want to put you to the trouble.'

'Oh, it's no trouble. No trouble.' Pettigrew unwedged himself and opened the door of a room which faced the garden. Swift looked over his shoulder but had no intention of going in. He had a strong suspicion that Pettigrew was now contemplating holding him there against his wishes.

'Oh, yes, I do like that room. I like it a great deal.' He edged around him in the pretence of getting a closer look, but as he did he saw that the wardrobe was open and there were clothes hanging in it. 'This is . . . is this your room?'

Pettigrew eyed the contents warmly. 'No. This is the Vincents' room. I told you.'

'But, according to the visitors' book, the Vincents were here in 1938.' Swift took a step backwards towards the stairs. His cheek broke a thick spider's web which folded around his mouth like candyfloss. As he tried to brush it off he winced from the contact of sharp scampering legs scuttling up his face and onto his head. His palm connected with the thick gritty body which crumbled like a small lump of coal into his hair. He shivered and a slither of something dropped down the back of his neck.

'1938. Yes.' Pettigrew shut the door and closed out the welcome light. Swift glimpsed a flash of silver in his palm. It looked like a blade among the heavy keys. He stumbled backwards and half tumbled, half ran down the stairs. He continued to run until he reached the bend in the road where he stopped to look back. Pettigrew's pale face was pressed to the filthy pane of the room at the end of the corridor. Swift set off to find Arnold and the woman.

Three

THE HOSPITAL

'You really shouldn't exert yourself.' A disembodied voice filtered through Swift's consciousness as he lay exhausted on his bed. He had a vague memory of chasing the tennis girl across the garden, then stumbling and falling, finally waking back on the ward. Lunch had been brought to him on a tin tray by the woman who had interrupted his first tennis game. She seemed to enjoy the spectacle of him lying prone and sweltering on the bed and made no attempt to help him sit up to eat the food. Instead she put the tray on the floor just out of his reach. When the doctor arrived Swift had been castigated for leaving the meal untouched.

'I was only running. Jogging really, hardly exerting myself.'

'And don't imagine you're in any fit state to leave.' The ownership of the voice became clear as Swift opened his eyes to see a doctor slipping the clipboard onto the end of the bed. It was the man from the room beside the cedar tree. 'Contrary to what you may believe, we do know best.'

'I should like to find my son. You can understand that, can't you?'

'Of course I understand it.' The doctor hoisted himself onto the bed and sat on his hands, his short legs barely reaching the floor. 'Except that you haven't yet mentioned a son to me.'

'Haven't I? I thought I had.'

'No. We've talked briefly about your wife, and the night of the raid, but at no time did you mention a son.' His mood had brightened. Like a detective, his interest had been renewed by the development in Swift's case.

'Yes, well, as you can imagine, finding my son is of paramount importance to me. An absolute priority.'

'Of course. Of course.' He smiled benignly.

'Then . . . then . . .' Swift tried, 'look, are you sure I haven't mentioned the boy?'

'Absolutely. Absolutely. What you reveal to yourself and what you reveal to me are quite separate although it's quite common to believe that they are in some way the same. My task is to enable you to distinguish between the two and simply learn to listen to yourself again.'

'So you're suggesting that I have only just revealed . . .'

'To yourself the existence of a son. Perhaps to protect yourself from the pain of revealing to him the death of his mother.'

'I don't think so.'

'Of course you don't. But that is merely one possibility. It could have been provoked by any number of factors. Perhaps it was cumulative — or perhaps it can be traced to that single traumatic night.'

'You're very fond of that word, "perhaps", aren't you?'

'Not at all. The understanding of the human psyche is an art, not a science, and for as long as it remains so we can only deal in probabilities and not certainties.' The man smiled secretively. 'There is a cure finding some favour abroad which involves the application of electricity. We've had some remarkable results in the short time we've used it here.' The threat was left hanging as the doctor looked conspiratorially towards a nurse reading a magazine at her table between the beds. Her starched scholastic profile was mirrored in the high sheen of the polished floor. The room was as spotless, silent and ordered as a library.

Swift tired of his view of the fan slowly revolving above his head, churning languidly through the stale hot air. 'How did I come here?' He watched the doctor watching the nameless sedated figure in the opposite bed.

'Your brother-in-law brought you. Patrick is it?'

'So we're close to Manchester, are we?'

'Yes. Ten miles. Is that important to you?'

'Not unduly.'

'Fine.' The doctor vaulted agilely from the bed; his leather soles landed like tap shoes on the tiled

117

floor. The nurse looked up, startled, then, on seeing the cause of the noise, smiled forgivingly. The doctor winked at her and her smile diluted.

'Do you live near here? Are you married?' Swift's hunger to know more about the man he was dealing with came from the sense that if he could just get a clear fix on the present it would be easier to retrace his own past.

'Yes, I live here. And no, I'm not married.' A discreet cough came from the nurse. 'Footloose and fancy free. A regular income, good prospects. I even have a car and coupons to run it.' The two men waited but no further response came from the table.

'I knew a nurse once. Did I tell you that?'

'Yes, you mentioned the woman on the train.' The doctor forced enthusiasm in his voice to prop up his flagging interest.

'Ah. Yes, I remember.' Swift's memory served him the image of Pettigrew at the hotel window. Then his frantic race to catch up with Arnold and the woman. 'Did we talk much about it?'

'A little.' The doctor returned his full attention to Swift.

'She was concerned that ... she was concerned somehow that we'd all perished in the raid, and the village was ...'

'Yes?'

'And the boy's name was Arnold which was odd considering that it's also the name of my son.'

'I see. Which would explain why you considered

the episode in which you left the train and found the village to have been a dream.'

'Did I?'

'That's what you said.'

'And was it?'

'Possibly. But you attach a great deal of significance to it, therefore it wouldn't do for us to dismiss it even if it was a dream. Indeed, if it was a dream it doesn't take any great leap of the imagination for us to interpret what you were indicating to yourself.'

'And if it wasn't?'

'Then perhaps the coincidence of the names together with the recent trauma added a certain gloss to your visit to the village and, in your mind, elevated the significance of it.'

'Perhaps.'

'Yes. Perhaps.'

Although what the doctor was telling Swift appealed to his logic, there remained a spiritual dimension to his visit to the village which he knew cold logic would never explain. At the core of it lay the woman's interpretation of their journey. He knew that his dismissive response to her differed little from the doctor's reaction to him. Like faith, there was a level which went beyond understanding and had simply to be accepted; analysis conferred rejection.

The doctor excused himself with a promise to return later in the afternoon. Swift had used what little energy he had left in their short conversation and lay back on the large pillows. When he closed his eyes and sleep overtook him his other life began again. The present, it seemed, had ceased to have any bearing on his future, beyond the moments within it that he spent contemplating his past. And as another reel began projecting itself through the white dust-specked light it was his past to which he again returned.

LONDON

THE city was sombre when Swift arrived back. He had left at the moment when excitement was still colouring the fear; like one's response to the first fall of snow: an optimism as yet uncoloured by the prosaic realities of black ice, sludge and burst pipes. In the short time he had been away it seemed to have been accepted that the war was not going to end overnight, that rationing was set to stay, that families were to be split by evacuation and that, however remote a possibility, German stormtroopers might, at any moment, appear from the skies. This, at least, was the interpretation of the young woman who was offering him a room to rent in

Battersea. Her husband had been conscripted three months before and her two children were now billeted with a family in Wales. She was to visit them in six weeks' time, and she was counting the days. She had recently taken in a lodger called Powers who lived in the back bedroom.

Swift listened patiently to the garbled biography as he waited like a child who had broken a window — at the step of the grey, terraced house, unprotected from the thin cold rain, with his sole earthly possessions in one of Dorothy's bags. The woman finally took breath, uncrossed her thick arms and ushered him into the dank hallway. She stood sideways to allow him past then darted a glance up and down the street before closing the door.

'I'll have to have your coupons. This way.' She led him into the small kitchen. A creel of washing was steaming in front of an open fire; the table was cluttered with spent matches, a pot of glue and an empty bottle. 'That's Powers' mess,' she said with a degree of resignation. 'Put your case down, if you're staying.' She looked Swift up and down. He knew it would be the last chance he had to decline the offer of the room and that the pot of tea she was now preparing effectively sealed the contract. But despite the clutter, the room was clean and the riot of domestic smells that assaulted him by no means unpleasant: baking pastry, washing-powder, carbolic soap. The woman smelt strongly of talcum powder, and as Swift passed her in the corridor he had breathed in the aroma greedily.

The kitchen and small back yard lay in the shadow of a railway viaduct but the clatter and distant thunder of passing trains held a peculiarly calming reassurance of normality. He put his case down and sat on one of the fragile wooden chairs at the table.

'No, that's Powers' chair. You can sit there.' She pointed the tea strainer at the chair opposite. 'He's very particular about his seat. Got any fags?'

Swift tamped a cigarette free of the packet and offered it to her. She took it elegantly between her thumb and first finger then spoilt his illusion by clamping it in the side of her mouth. He offered her a light in his cupped palm so that she was forced to bend towards him. She held back her long straight dark hair with both of her hands as she suckled at the orange flame. 'Ta.' She inhaled and exhaled without removing the cigarette, half closing her right eye to protect it from the smoke. 'Mr Swift then is it?'

'Yes. Call me Gregory if you like.'

'No. I wouldn't like. Best to keep things nice and formal. You can call me Mrs Miller. It's Joyce. But call me Mrs Miller.'

'All right, Mrs Miller.'

She smiled flirtatiously. 'No. It doesn't sound right, does it? Call me Joyce, when we're ... you know, when we're in the house.' She turned away to hide her embarrassment.

Swift was strongly attracted to the woman. She was large framed but carried her size easily. Her haughtiness had quickly softened towards him in the oven-warm kitchen. Her face seemed incapable of hiding anything — which, he assumed, was why she sought refuge in giving him details of her family. He knew she was a woman he could easily hurt, and the infliction of pain on somebody else was an option he had not recently enjoyed.

'What will your husband say about you taking in a lodger?'

'Oh, he won't bother,' she laughed warmly. 'He can't see the harm in anybody. Anyway, I've already got Powers. But he doesn't count.'

Swift took the cup of tea and cradled it between his palms. 'And can you?'

'Me? Oh, I can see enough harm for both of us. That's why . . .' She pinched out her cigarette and laid it in the ashtray. 'Look, are you going to take the room? Only, if you're not I've got things to be getting on with.'

'Yes. I should like to.' Swift stood in an attempt to reintroduce the formality to the contract. 'Do we shake hands? I'm sorry, I haven't done this before.'

'We'll settle at the end of each week and take it from there if you like.' Mrs Miller held out her hand and Swift clasped it.

'That suits me.'

'And I'd like to know something about you, Mr Swift. That way when the police come knocking I can have a story ready.' She laughed but Swift saw she was watching closely for his reaction.

'Don't worry, Joyce, you won't get any trouble from me.' He dropped in the familiarity self-consciously.

'Good. I'll show you the way if you like.' She waited for him to lead her into the hallway and up the stairs, suspicious enough not to turn her back on him. At the top he walked into the first room on the landing. Two beds were made up; a wooden chest of children's toys was squared away beneath a table, the shelves stacked neatly with books regimented by height, their spines pristine. 'You can choose a bed. The bathroom's next door, the privy's in the yard. We eat at six. All right?'

'Fine. Thank you. I'm sure I'll be very comfortable here.'

Mrs Miller looked once more round the room before leaving him to unpack; the ghosts of her children bounced on the mattresses, refusing sleep. She pictured them huddled together for warmth in a drafty Welsh farmhouse and shivered.

'Powers, do you want a cup of tea!' The woman shouted the offer then tugged the door closed behind her. Swift heard a mumbled reply then her footsteps on the stairs. From the window he could see into the bare bulb-lit lime green bedroom of the house that backed onto their small yard. Its windows were latticed with tape, the room looked like a dingy theatrical set, waiting for a murder to be committed and the action to begin. In the distance, towards Victoria, the tall funnels of the power station stretched into the grey sky. Above them, incongruous as flying pigs, the barrage balloons rippled and bobbed on taut steel hawsers. The misty rain had stopped; back doors were opening along the terrace as women emerged tentatively with baskets of washing. Without exception they glanced towards the balloons, judging their height, gaining reassurance from their presence. The higher the better; superstition dictated that when the balloons were high there would be no raid.

Swift dropped the net curtain and opened Dorothy's bag on the bed. He removed the pristine pile of Patrick's underclothes and put them on the table, then he sat on the bed and wept.

*

An hour later, prompted by loneliness, he went downstairs again, intending to pick up the conversation with his landlady. Instead he found a man he concluded to be Powers at the kitchen table gluing matches together with the aid of a small pair of pincers and a magnifying glass.

Powers was broad shouldered and built like a middleweight boxer. He was hunched like a retarded child over the construction on the tray which looked like an abstract representation of a volcano, flecked with small pieces of torn newspaper. The man was so absorbed by his model-making that Swift waited a full two minutes before being noticed. When he was, and Swift introduced himself, the man shook his hand without looking up and informed him that he was two hours early for dinner. Swift, picking the cow gum from his fingers, sat down and offered his tentative interpretation of the man's endeavours. 'Volcano?'

Powers squinted at the model, then turned it round and peered at it from another angle. 'No, I can't see that. I can't see that at all.' He returned to his endeavours with the precision of a philatelist and pasted another fistful of matches to the top of the pile. 'If you can't see it I'm not going to tell you what it is.'

'Joyce . . .' Swift began, then waited until he'd hooked Powers' attention.

'I heard you.'

'It must be hard for her to be separated from her children.'

Powers looked up. 'Must it?'

'I would have thought so.'

Powers looked at his watch. 'You've been here how long?'

'I'm sorry, it was just a . . . I was merely . . .'

'Put the kettle on, will you.' Powers waved him away with irritation.

'Of course.' Swift lit the gas ring then rinsed the

tea cups that were standing on the drainer. The man was completely absorbed by his task, the mountain of matches growing with no discernible purpose.

'There!' Powers rubbed his hands on a sheet of newspaper and looked gleefully at the woeful construction.

'I'm sorry,' Swift confided, 'I'm not at all well versed in the abstract.'

'Abstract. Wossat? Try again.' He turned the tray round ninety degrees and offered it with a magician's flourish. 'There!'

'I'm sorry. I haven't a clue.'

'Give me ten bob and I'll tell you.'

'That's a little steep for information I have absolutely no interest in obtaining.'

'Call it a tanner then.'

Swift fished in his pocket and sifted through his change. Sixpence seemed a reasonable price to prevent any further pestering. 'Here.' He chinked the coin into the saucer and handed Powers his tea.

'It's the Eiffel Tower.' He looked up, beaming. 'Get it?'

'No. I'm sorry, I still can't see it.'

'You think it's rubbish, don't you?'

'Well . . .'

Powers crashed his fist down, shattering the model and sending splintered matches across the table. 'Of course it's rubbish, but it earnt me a tanner didn't it?' Powers smiled, victorious. 'Careless talk cost you a tanner. Get it?'

Swift sipped his tea.

'Yaah.' Powers tugged down his shirt sleeves and anchored his cuffs together with large gold links. He was a dapper man with a carrion face. Brutality lurked beneath the surface of his shallow smile; his heavily muscled arms strained the shoulders of his immaculate cotton shirt. Powers put on his jacket and ran his finger round the collar of his shirt. 'Look.' He stretched to his full height which was, surprisingly, a little under Swift's, and stood intimidatingly close, trapping him against the oven. 'Look.' He pressed a powerful index finger upwards against Swift's Adam's apple. 'I don't care about you coming here. I don't give a toss. Just so long as you keep out of my hair ... all right?' He feigned a punch, pulling it just short of Swift's face, then brushed his Brylcreemed hair flat with the follow-through. 'Get it?'

'Yes.' Swift swallowed drily.

'You want to get yourself a tattoo. Here.' He reached up and ran his finger across Swift's forehead. 'Nice bird like. Chicken or something, pecking at little bits of corn in your eyebrows. What do you think?'

'I think I might need some time to consider that suggestion.' Swift smiled weakly. The life had gone out of Powers' eyes. He shook his head and it returned.

'I think you're raving mad.' Powers backed off, then slumped back into the chair. 'Why did you have to come here anyway?'

'I came here to find my son.'

'Why? Did you lose him?'

'Yes.' Swift had no intention of revealing anything further to Powers. He could deal with the man's thuggery, but he knew he could not bear having the purpose of his journey subjected to brutal scrutiny.

'Some people'd lose their heads if they weren't screwed on.'

'It wasn't like that.'

'No?'

'No.'

'Fair enough. I'm going out. Tell her I'll be back for my grub.' Powers thrust out his hand again. Swift recoiled. 'Shake on it then.' Swift shook the moist hand then Powers charged out through the back door. The yard gate crashed open against the privy wall and remained open as Powers' footsteps diminished down the back alley. Swift brushed a chair clear of broken matches and sat down. Finally boredom prompted him to search for a brush and dustpan to clear up the remainder of Powers' mess. When the landlady came in with a full leather shopping bag he was kneeling beneath the table finishing off.

'I like to see a man doing something useful.' Swift looked up and banged his head on the underside of the table. 'Come out, you look like a dog in a kennel down there.'

Swift slid out backwards. 'I was clearing up the matches.'

'Then you'll have met Powers.' Like a mother confiscating a toy from a child, the woman took the brush and full dustpan away from him.

'Yes.'

'Powers is all right,' she said, dealing a pre-emptive blow for his defence.

'I'm sure he is.'

'He's been very good to me since my man went away.'

'He seemed very . . . capable.'

'Yes. He is capable. Very.' The reiteration put Swift firmly in his place. 'You can help me with these if you haven't got anything better to do with your time.'

Mrs Miller turned a brown paper bag of muddy potatoes bouncing into the sink and handed Swift a short-bladed knife. He ran the cold tap hard then immersed his hands beneath the shock of the icy water. His wrists began to numb, cooling the blood in his veins. Mrs Miller watched the ritual with curiosity. 'You haven't given me your alibi yet. For when the police come knocking.'

'No.' Swift was rapt by the texture of the potatoes in his cold hands. He weighed one in each, feeling blindly the gritty surface, probing the mud away with his thumb nails, forcing the dirt into his fingers.

'Have you lost the knife then, Mr Swift?' Mrs Miller was suddenly next to him, her hand plunging between his like a fish. The charge of the contact sent a shock through his body. Her hand grasped the knife and lingered beneath the water. Swift looked at the woman but she was gazing out of the window at the yard gate swinging in the breeze to the echo of Powers' departure. He felt as though he had ownership neither of his hands nor of his emotions. He took her wrist and held it. She allowed the contact without protesting then gently pulled away bringing the knife to the surface of the thick brown water. 'There.' She dashed the knife dry and handed it back to him. Swift couldn't tell whether the woman hadn't registered the contact or had simply chosen to ignore it.

'There's a shelter at the end of the street. I should have told you that, in case I'm out.'

'Thank you.' Swift swallowed drily.

'I hate it in there. It stinks. I don't go in it myself. All that singing.'

'Thank you.'

'I prefer the underground. Powers prefers the underground too.'

'Does he?'

'He cries like a baby sometimes, you should hear him. I don't mind. Look, are you all right?' Mrs Miller was peering closely at Swift who had frozen at the sink, unable to withdraw his hands from the water.

'You should use the shelter. You have responsibilities towards your children.'

'Yes, I know I should. I can bear the stink. I just can't stand the music.' She gently tried to move him aside. 'Look, let me do those. You sit down, you've had a long journey today, haven't you?'

'Thank you.' With a huge force of effort Swift removed his hands from the water and sat at Powers' seat at the table. The woman took his place at the sink.

'You didn't say where you'd come from.'

'From Manchester. I came down last night. I came to find my son.'

'Your son?' Mrs Miller turned from the sink, but continued peeling the potatoes. 'I didn't know you had a boy.'

'Yes. Arnold. His name is Arnold.'

'I see.' She paused as she examined how she could use the information.

'I have to find him.'

'Of course you do. You should get Powers on to it, he's good at finding things.' She turned back to her task. 'He's a very capable man, Powers.'

'So you said, but I'd rather leave him out of it if you wouldn't mind.'

'No. You can suit yourself.' The scraping of potato skins bridged the silence. 'You came down from Manchester then did you?'

'Yes. From my sister's house. She has two boys.'

'That's nice.'

'I thought I should get back and . . . I don't know, just get on with it.'

'With finding your boy.'

'Yes. Exactly. Exactly.'

'Well, there's no time like tomorrow as Powers says.'

'Do you mind if I ask how he came to be here?'

'No, I don't mind.' Mrs Miller carried a large pan from the stove to the sink and began dropping in the potatoes. 'He was a trainer you see.'

'Yes?'

'Well my husband — Don — he worked for a bookie for a while, it's a long story, he's a joiner really, but he was working for this bookie in Clapham and he got to know Powers then. I never asked him how he came to be mixing with that side of things, but he met him and then Powers invited him down to Brighton races a couple of times. They were great friends really. Dusty thought the world of Powers.'

'Dusty?'

'Don. Yes. Don. There.' Mrs Miller filled the pan with water and set it on the stove. 'Right. We can have five minutes then I'll have to get on. Woolton Pie. You'll have to take what you get, only I do it a bit different. Powers likes it.' She took the seat beside him at the table. 'When he was bombed out you see, it seemed only right that I should put him up.'

'Of course.'

'Tell me about your boy.' The woman had softened her tone and Swift felt safe enough with her to confide.

'It's a long story.'

'All right, you can have ten minutes.' She smiled a gentle smile, her eyes creased with genuine warmth.

'He's ah . . . he's eleven years old.'

'Two years older than my oldest. Go on.'

'He's a studious boy.'

'Clever you mean.'

'No, but he tries. He tries.'

'Go on.'

'I'm sorry. I can't.' Swift barely got the words out before the tears came again, rushing like an avalanche through his emotions, carrying all his rationality away in its path.

'There.' Mrs Miller made no move towards him, but her tone allowed him the permission to lay his forehead on her shoulder as he wept. 'There.' Swift felt her hand caressing the back of his head, the nails hard against his scalp, and long after his pain subsided she continued, her breathing changing its rhythm, the pressure of her touch more firm.

He lay against her until her hand was snatched away and he felt her pushing him roughly off.

Immediately afterwards the back door crashed open and Powers came in.

'There's word of a nun parachuting in with hairy legs.' Powers was panting with the news.

'That's twice I've heard that this week.' Mrs Miller went back to the stove, leant down and lit the oven with a match.

'She was dreaming of Hitler last night,' Powers said with glee, tossing a look in the woman's direction.

'I told you that confidentially,' the woman chided.

Swift watched the domestic exchange with little pleasure. Somehow Powers was even more obnoxious than he had been before and his landlady had adopted a flirtatious tone.

'Don't know what good he'd be to you. Only having one bollock an' that.' Powers winked at Swift. 'Here.' He drew out a packet of cigarettes from his inside pocket and threw them on the table. 'Pashas, it's all I could get.'

'Thanks.' Mrs Miller greeted the arrival of the Turkish cigarettes with little enthusiasm.

'I'm not queueing up all day.' Powers cast his attention round the room like a bully looking for a victim. 'Put the kettle on, will you?'

'Put it on yourself. I'm not your slave.'

'That's not what you said last night.' Powers guffawed.

'Don't flatter yourself.'

'Hey,' Powers said, 'I heard they were starting a new campaign.'

'Did you?' The landlady was dusting a tray with flour.

'Yeah, apparently they're going to flatten Wales now and leave us alone.' He winked again, soliciting Swift's approval.

'That's not funny, Powers. That's not funny at all.' The woman brushed her hands on her apron and went out into the yard.

'Don't do it, Mother — leave the kiddies where they are! Have you seen the poster?' Powers fired the question at Swift but didn't wait for a reply. 'She's very touchy about her kids.' Powers' stage whisper could have been heard next door.

'I think I might go and have a rest.' Swift excused himself and went to the door.

'Yeah, you don't want to overdo it, do you? Something I said, was it?'

After Swift left the room he heard Powers follow the woman into the yard and the beginning of an apology. The sound of them both was cut off when he shut the bedroom door and lay on the bed. He was exhausted. The early train had taken over seven hours to reach London. It had detoured somewhere in the Midlands where the line had been ruptured by a stray bomb from an aircraft limping towards the Channel. The train had been packed with soldiers but their mood had been ugly and Swift had chosen not to leave his seat for fear of drawing attention to himself. A woman had come into the compartment for part of the journey and the soldiers had verbally assaulted her with risqué suggestions until she left. Swift felt himself fully implicated in the attack as he had made no attempt to defend her, but he had neither the physical nor the emotional strength for heroics. When the woman finally got off it was to Swift she mouthed abuse through the window. It was this disquieting image of hate that he carried with him into his sleep.

THE VILLAGE

SWIFT left the village and walked briskly back towards the station. He had expected to catch up with Arnold and the woman but as he turned into the station lane he had seen neither of them. Only as he hurried onto the platform did he find them, Arnold tiptoeing along the platform edge, a tightrope walker's shadow cast by the high sun onto the ground. The woman was smoking a cigarette on the bench, watching the boy's antics with pride.

The smoke rose and dissipated slowly in the still air.

'There you are.' Swift sagged breathlessly onto the bench.

'We thought you'd decided to stay with the egg man.' The woman studied him coolly.

'No. No, I didn't.' Swift checked that Arnold was out of earshot and leant towards the woman. 'I think he was a little unhinged.'

'Well, we did try to tell you, didn't we?'

'Any sign of a train?'

'Yes. I spoke to the little man in the hut and he seems to think there's one due within the hour.'

'Really?'

'Yes, really.'

'That's good. Isn't it?'

'Absolutely bloody marvellous, Mr Bowler. Marvellous.' She turned away from him, and then, as if she could no longer stand being close to him, walked sharply away tugging her coat round her. Swift followed, angry at being subjected to her anger without, he believed, deserving it.

'Look.' He tried to take her arm, she shook him off.

'What!'

'Look, what's wrong?'

'I thought it was obvious.'

'No. Tell me.'

'I don't want to go back.' Her eyes blazed with tears and anger.

'I'm sorry.'

'Oh, don't apologise. Please don't apologise.'

'It wasn't an apology. It's not my fault.'

'I didn't say it was your fault. Why do you assume everything is always about you?'

'Because . . . because in a way I think it is.'

'Well it's not. What concern of yours could it possibly be that I have nowhere to stay?'

'You should have told me.'

'I say again, Mr Bowler, and this time please listen: this is not about you.'

'Then I apologise. But if there is anything I can do please don't hesitate to ask.'

'You sound like the manager of a cheap hotel.' The woman laughed shrilly. Arnold looked round, missing his footing and just catching his balance before plunging onto the tracks.

'I suppose you'd know about cheap hotels.' Swift lashed out without thinking. His cheek smarted as the blow from her palm struck him.

'That was callous.'

The pleasure of having provoked a response from the woman led Swift to pursue her with cruelty. 'And you're too wrapped up in yourself to have any inkling as to what is going on in the mind of anyone else.'

'That is not true!'

'Oh, I'm sorry to say that it certainly is.'

'How dare you!'

'I must say I can't ever imagine you passing

muster as a nurse. I'm not surprised you left, I'm really not.' Swift warmed to his theme. Offloading his pain he found profoundly therapeutic.

The woman looked at him with shock. She mouthed a reply but no words came out.

'Don't tell me you're lost for words.' He looked to Arnold for approval but the boy looked equally disturbed. 'What's the matter, Arnold? Cat got your tongue?'

'Leave him alone.' The woman, sensing danger from Swift, forced herself to regain control.

'Why? He can talk for himself, can't he?' Swift raised his voice. 'I said you can talk for yourself, can't you, boy?'

'Yes sir,' Arnold replied weakly. He was frozen between moving to the woman to protect her and staying where he was to protect himself. The man he knew as 'Swift' or 'Mr Bowler' who had been kind enough to allow him along was gone. In his place was a monster of headmasterly proportions.

'I said leave him alone!' The woman resolved Arnold's quandary by going to him and wrapping her arm around his shoulders.

'Very well. Very well.' Swift walked a small circle, hands pocketed, his attention fixed on the floor. Having completed it he looked up to see the woman and child still locked together. 'Yes?'

'We didn't say anything.' The woman's shock had quickly become defiance. She held her head a little higher. There was something in her eyes which

Swift knew he could not defeat; her focus was fixed on a distant point. He recognised the evangelical stare from their walk to the village just the day before, which now seemed a lifetime away. The purpose of protecting Arnold defined her more clearly to him, just as had the purpose of finding the village. He understood a little more how the loss of the child on the night ward had devastated her. Her strength of purpose implied a strength of will; if her will could not save a child then how could she save herself?

Swift expected no forgiveness as he began his apology. The woman swallowed the bitter taste of his words and accepted it.

*

They sat in the waiting-room like victims of a ship-wreck for the boat home, aware that what had grown between them would not survive the transposition to their other lives and all silently preparing themselves for the farewells. The woman scrawled an address on a piece of paper, folded it like a secret note and handed it to Swift with the explanation that it was her London address, and when she could bear it she would eventually be returning there, war permitting. Arnold, seeing this, drew out a dog-eared stub of pencil from his pocket and wrote his own address on a sweet wrapper which he then gave to the woman. Swift's heart sank with the pathos of the act. Arnold then found the door to the ticket office and scouted off to explore the parts of the station previously denied him.

'He's a good boy,' the woman said.

'Yes. Yes, considering the circumstances he's not been a burden, has he?'

'No.'

'You could come to Manchester you know. I'm sure my sister would be happy to let you have a room until you get something sorted out.' Swift's tone continued to be apologetic. Until they were removed from the setting he knew he would not be able to apologise enough. More than that, his attack had scorched so deep into his memory that, each time he stepped onto a station platform, he would remember it. But he was feeling profoundly unwell. He blinked back the mist that was clouding his eyes but his forehead was heavy and seemed to be exerting pressure on his eyebrows. The detour to the village had allowed him to forget his grief, but now it had returned: sharper; uncluttered by shock.

'No. Thank you but no.' The woman gently waved away his offer.

The distant rumble of a train made the breath catch in Swift's throat. Despite the fact that he knew they would be travelling together for at least the next hour or so he felt keenly that what he wanted to say needed to be said in the village. The train carriage belonged in a separate context: of normality and longing, where new life and hope were stunted beneath the long shadow of the war.

A signal squeaked and clattered down at the end of the platform. Arnold appeared at the ticket hatch waiting for the instruction to go out onto the platform; the return to civilisation meant the loss of free will.

'I suppose we ought to go.' The woman led the way out into the light. The sun burnt down on them; Arnold shielded his eyes and looked directly towards it.

'I think I might come and find you,' Swift said. 'When things are . . . well, a little more settled.'

'I wouldn't mind that. And I do hope you find your son.'

'Yes. I shall. I'm sure I shall.'

They stood in uncomfortable silence as the train took an eternity to appear and then lumber towards them along the platform.

'I don't think you can make any decisions until you find him.' The woman was watching Arnold again, preparing herself for the separation.

'Help me,' Swift said.

'Help you? What on earth do you mean?'

'I don't know.'

'I can't, Mr Bowler. You can only help yourself.'

The train slid to a stop, nobody got off, and Swift, Arnold and the woman were the only ones to join it. A whistle cut shrilly through the silence. The train jolted and slowly moved away.

THE HOSPITAL

'**D**OROTHY. It's Gregory.' It was mid afternoon, Swift was borrowing the telephone in the hospital's administrative office. An owlish woman was typing in the small space and Swift was forced to raise his voice over the clatter of the machine. The woman returned the carriage vigorously so that Swift had to time his sentences to the metre of her line breaks. 'I've decided to leave. Dorothy... hello ... sorry, I thought I'd lost the line. I'm going back to London. There seems little point in remaining here... I met the doctor again... yes, he seemed perfectly well intentioned but rather... I'm sorry?...' The typing stopped, the paper and carbon were snatched noisily from the ratchet of the roller, the typist peered over her half-moon glasses at Swift, challenging him to complain. He turned his back on her; the tennis girl walked past the open door and mimed an underarm serve; Swift mimed a return. '... Yes, I thought I'd let you know. I'll call you in a day or so... that's fine. Look, I'm borrowing a telephone. I have to go. Love to the boys.'

Swift returned to the ward and began to pack his few possessions in the bag Dorothy had lent him. He was aware of being watched by the nurse at her table, but when he was fully packed he looked towards her desk and she was gone.

'They won't let you go, you know.' The tennis girl had appeared and was watching him from her position just inside the ward door.

'Are you allowed in here?' Swift turned his back on her to do up his trousers; when he looked round she was rifling through a sheaf of papers at the nurse's desk.

'Oh, I can go anywhere I like. I can do anything I want to do.'

'I would have thought it unwise to wander through the wards.'

'Would you?' The girl went to the bed beside the desk and peered closely at the figure sleeping on it.

'Yes. I would. For all sorts of reasons.'

'They won't let you go, you know,' the girl repeated smugly.

'Why not?' Swift decided to indulge her one last time before leaving.

'Because you might be dangerous.'

'Don't be ridiculous.'

'All right, don't believe me.' The girl made to go, but Swift called her back. She had not lied to him since he had arrived there and he had no reason to believe that she should start lying now.

'Tell me what you mean.'

'That's what they say. That you might be dangerous — to yourself or to others. That's what they said
about Mother.'

'I can't imagine they'd have any such fear about
me.' Swift's laugh rang hollowly through the ward.
The long gap in his memory prompted his lack of
conviction.

'I'm sure that's what my mother thought. My
sister couldn't stand it. That's why she left. She
couldn't bear to see what they did to Mother.'

Swift's mind went back to the bad-tempered conversation on the tennis court which had culminated
in the older girl flouncing off. He had not seen her
since.

'And what did they do to your mother?'

'They injected her with something, then they
attached something to her head and fat Desmond
switched something and Mummy jumped up as
though they'd stuck a huge needle into her side. He
smells, doesn't he?'

'That sounds quite terrible.' Swift now had only
one concern: he knew he had to get out of the hospital before 'Fat Desmond', as the child had christ-
ened him, offered him a dose of the same treatment.
He knew now why the nurse had disappeared when
he began his packing.

'And now she's . . . it's as though she's not there.
I don't think she knows who I am. And now they're
talking about operating on her brain — I heard

them talking. I hear everything. They think I'm too young. But I hear everything.'

'And have you heard them talking about me?'

'Yes.' The girl fixed her attention on her feet.

'Come on. Please. I don't think there's much time.'

'Oh. They're going to do the same. Desmond says you're . . . oh, I can't remember what he said. He doesn't like you. None of them likes you. I don't suppose that matters but I think it's unkind.'

'I have to go.' He kissed the child on the cheek.

'Yes. Goodbye.'

Swift took his bag from the bed then walked hurriedly towards the back staircase. As he reached the door he heard two or three sets of footsteps approaching the ward. He froze then tore open the door and sprinted down the stone stairs. The door banged open above him and he heard a shout echoing down the narrow stairwell; the followers began to run, their leather soles scuffing the steps. Swift reached the bottom, opened the door, then made left along the corridor towards the administrative office and the main hospital entrance. He ran into a nurse and sent her sprawling, then mumbled an apology before tearing on along the long corridor. Just before he reached the reception the voice of fat Desmond brought him up short. Swift stopped, leaning on the wall for support while he got his breath back. The doctor was ordering those with him to patrol the front and rear exits of the hospital.

There was no sense of urgency in the man's voice, it was clear that he considered it only a matter of time before Swift was caught. His arrogance hardened Swift's resolve to get away. He had no intention of being subjected to Desmond's experimental cure.

'Quick. This way!' The tennis girl appeared behind him at the bend in the corridor. Swift waited for her to be joined by Desmond's followers but none came. He followed her unquestioningly, tiptoeing along the corridor, he with heart beating hard, she hugging the wall, frantic with excitement.

'In here.' The child opened a door and led him into the familiar warmth of the boiler room. The door closed behind them and they stood in the darkness like foxes in a hole waiting for Desmond to appear. After five minutes Swift relaxed and began plotting his escape from the garden to the nearby station. The child whispered to him details of a route which he could negotiate without needing to go back through the main building. He felt his way towards the boilers, but as he reached the rail, the corridor door was snatched open and Desmond stood framed in the square of light.

'There you are.'

'I have decided to leave.' Swift summoned all the authority he felt he possessed. 'You can't keep me here against my will.'

'Of course we can't.' Desmond was a study in reasonableness.

'Very well then.' Swift tried the garden door. It

opened and he climbed the stone steps out into the light. He reached the tennis court without looking back and felt his tension begin to diminish. The child had told him that the station lay beyond the far line of trees at the edge of the garden and he strode towards them clutching Dorothy's bag. His instinct was to run but his pride prevented him. Half way across the lawn his progress was halted by an iron grip on his arm. He swung round to protest, but as he did so something was plunged into his shoulder. The far line of saplings weaved like a wave, the silence crowded in on him and he blacked out.

Four

LONDON

SWIFT awoke feeling feverish and disorientated. It took him a while to get a bearing on the room and only when he looked out at the house behind did he remember where he was. He went downstairs and found Powers and the landlady in the kitchen. Powers was frowning at the headlines in the paper, the words forming slowly on his lips. The landlady was smoking a Turkish cigarette, leaning boredly against the sink. A pot was bubbling on the stove, the back door was open and the smoke from the woman's cigarette stealing out into the fresh air. 'How are you feeling?' Mrs Miller said and Swift was cheered by the fact that she seemed genuinely pleased to see him.

'I'm fine. Fine . . .'

'Was the bed all right for you?'

'Very comfortable.' Swift stretched theatrically.

Powers looked up, cross at the intrusion, then returned to his newspaper.

'Dinner won't be long now.' Mrs Miller flicked the ash of her cigarette expertly round the frame of the door and into the yard. Swift sat at the table which had been laid with three sets of bone-handled cutlery. An HP sauce bottle stood by the salt and pepper pots at the centre of the table.

'It smells good.' Swift felt he was being called on to play the role of invited dinner guest rather than the more prosaic one of lodger.

'I hope so,' Mrs Miller said.

'So do I,' Powers contributed without taking his eyes from the paper.

'Powers is cross,' the woman said. 'I think he's jealous. Are you jealous, Powers?'

'Sod off.'

'He's jealous. He likes having me all to himself and now you've come along . . . he doesn't like that.'

Powers didn't reply but his grip tightened on the newspaper.

'I don't think he has anything to fear,' Swift said. 'I'm sure I won't be under your feet for very long.'

'Oh she won't like that. She won't like that at all.' Powers turned a page of his paper then folded it back on itself as he delivered his opinion.

'He doesn't know anything,' the woman said. 'He just likes stirring people up.' She flicked the nub of her cigarette out into the yard then turned the gas down on the stove. 'It's ready now. If you'd like to wash your hands.'

Swift trooped obediently to the sink, happy to play his part. Powers creased his paper in half and slipped it into his jacket pocket then picked up his knife and fork in readiness for the meal.

*

They ate in silence, Swift's appetite dented by Powers' slovenly open-mouthed consumption of the pie. Any items that dropped back onto his plate he forced back onto his fork with his little finger before cramming it back into his mouth.

'So you're looking for your boy then, are you?' Powers said, after the meal was over.

Swift tensed and concurred.

'I don't think Mr Swift wants to talk about that, Powers.' The landlady threw him a wounding look but Powers pursued his point.

'You're a bit of a mystery, aren't you?'

'I wouldn't say so.'

'Oh. I think you are. I know a few rum types and you wouldn't stand out in a crowd of them.'

'Thank you. But I really don't think it's any of your business.' Swift had yet to devise a strategy for handling Powers and he was annoyed with himself.

'You could be a Bolshie for all we know.' Powers looked to the woman for confirmation.

'Don't be stupid.'

'Well he could. Where's his luggage, then? Where's his papers?'

'I have my papers,' Swift said coolly. 'And my clothes were destroyed in the bombing.'

'Yeah, well that's what you say. And all this malarkey about your lad. I personally think it's a load of balls.'

'I really don't care what you think. Your opinion is of no interest to me whatsoever.'

'Powers,' the woman said, 'you can see Mr Swift doesn't want to talk about it, so why don't you leave it alone.'

'I don't see why I should let him get away with saying something like that. It's bloody rude — all that opinion — and what he said. Why should he be allowed to say things like that? Eh?'

'You started it. Now you can stop it.' The woman began collecting the plates. Swift handed his to her, Powers brushed his aside, and pulled the ashtray towards him.

'Bloody rude I say,' Powers said under his breath.

'Let me help you with those,' Swift followed the woman to the sink.

'Oh my God! He wants to do the washing up now.' Powers addressed an invisible audience. 'He'll be at the laundry tub next. Here,' he began undoing his braces, 'you can have my long johns, they could do with a good scrub.'

'You'll be looking for another room if you don't stop it.'

'I was only joking.' Powers sat meekly and took out his cigarette case. 'Some people just can't take a joke.'

Mrs Miller began washing the pots, Swift dried

each one as it was handed to him. The blackout curtain blocked out the night; the door was now shut, the room claustrophobic. Swift wanted to leave; to run to the village, to find the woman and Arnold, to sit in the silent waiting-room waiting for the train, even to be back in the scarred church waiting for the pallbearers to arrive. He belonged nowhere, he felt utterly adrift and clung helplessly to his one remaining hope — that he could find his son and begin it all again.

The day of the funeral dropped like a shroud over his thoughts. The service over, he stood alone in the cratered graveyard watching a dogfight draw vapour trail hoops in the sea blue sky. He willed victory to the Spitfire snapping at the heels of the Messerschmitt. For Swift, and everyone who craned their necks to the sky, the airborne fight represented all that the powers deemed it necessary to know about the war. The forces of good pursued the forces of evil and when evil was vanquished the debris of its destruction was washed up on a distant beach, too far away for any human cost to be counted. The diagram was drawn day after day until it was understood well enough for the battle in the sky to become redundant.

The planes spiralled away. The Spitfire gave chase then peeled off and turned towards the north. Swift leant on a gravestone for support. He longed for the vicar to come out and offer him some words of comfort, or even for the plug-eared boy to cycle past so that he could be reminded of the future. But no-one came to help so he walked away and took the underground the two stops back to the remains of his house. When he climbed the steps back into the light and turned into the street, although he'd tried to prepare himself for the scene, it nevertheless came as a shock. The wrecked house had been cordoned off; those remaining standing on each side of the gap were shored up by timber to prevent the terrace collapsing. The windows were boarded over but the front door was open in the one house that seemed still to be inhabited. A group of children were sifting through the rubble looking for cartridge cases or shrapnel. When Swift shouted, they scattered like rats to regroup at a broken pram at the far end of the street.

Swift skirted the cordon and picked his way over the rubble. A curtain rail with a rag of fabric hanging loose from the end protruded through the mud like a fallen standard. He tried to pull it out but it was stuck fast. An armchair was upended; he righted it but it was filthy and broken; mirror glass crunched under his foot; he knelt to scrabble a picture frame from the ground but as he lifted it it came apart in his hands.

'Swift! There you are.' He heard the large and familiar voice of a neighbour. Donald Horsley's voice had always been an unwanted intrusion. Horsley was a bore; he lived two doors up the street with his equally tedious wife. But theirs was a thick-skinned boorishness, insensitive as Jehovah's Witnesses to all but the most blatant attack. Resentment towards them in the street was compounded by the fact that Horsley owned a small grocer's shop, and it was clear that they never did without. Horsley bumbled over the rubble like a huge beetle, stumbling to all fours then picking himself up with the particular grace of the obese. He was wearing a black sleeveless sweater over his tieless shirt, and his pin-striped trousers barely made the distance to his shoes. His face shone like a ruddy apple, perpetually perspiring, and he maintained a schoolboyish enthusiasm that Swift always ached to dent. Horsley arrived, having successfully negotiated the pile of earth and shattered belongings.

'You could have knocked.' Swift's admonishment allowed no response but Horsley nevertheless jacked his head round to check that by some fluke the door was not still standing.

'Shocking. Absolutely shocking.' Horsley looked at the destruction with the selfish eyes of a survivor.

'Did you escape it?'

'Not entirely. Not entirely I have to say. The dust is unbelievable. Mona's in despair over the carpets.'

'I'm sorry to hear that.'

'Thank you, Swift.' The irony was squandered on him. 'What do you ... I mean what will you do?'

'Oh, I don't know. I shall go and see my sister for a few days ... then, I don't know ... I just don't really know. I mean I've been at the rest centre for a few days but it's hardly ideal.'

'You could come and stay with us.' The Horsleys were notorious for collecting visitors and entrapping them for a period far longer than they intended to stay.

'No. I think, I mean I promised Dorothy I'd go and see them. To put them in the picture.'

'Of course. But the offer remains open.'

'Thank you.'

'Did the ... ah ... the funeral go off all right?' Horsley anchored his hands behind his back, a sign, Swift recognised, that he was preparing to dig himself in for a substantial conversation.

'Yes ... as well as I imagine any funerals are going off at the moment.'

'Yes. I saw the digging.' It took Swift a second to realise that Horsley was referring to the night of the raid and not to the funeral service. He looked towards Swift with what Swift took to be a plea for approval. Receiving only a hollow stare, he pressed on. 'Yes, I saw them. And then when they discovered ... well, you know, I called Mona out. Yes, we watched it all.'

'You watched it.'

'Yes. Quite ... extraordinary. Mona couldn't sleep at all that night.'

'I imagine she must have been utterly distraught.' Swift felt as though he was observing the conversation from above. He was unsure why he was egging Horsley on in his insensitivity but he realised he was getting a peculiar thrill from the anticipation of just how he was going to puncture his pomposity. It came to him that the destruction of his property and the death of his spouse severed both major ties to social conformity.

'Dreadfully distraught. Mona, as I imagine I don't have to remind you, prides herself on her tidiness. She tossed and turned and I knew, I knew without needing to ask her, that she feared for her ornaments. You've seen them?'

'I have. Yes.' Swift shuffled on his feet, the glass crunched underfoot. 'And I'm sorry that we had to put Mona to so much distress.'

'Oh, don't think I was suggesting . . .' Horsley laughed, inviting Swift to join him. When he caught the look on his face the laugh was cut short.

'Then what were you suggesting?'

'I wasn't suggesting anything Swift. I was . . .'

'I always knew you were a fool.'

Horsley swallowed a mouthful of air. The group of children sensed the mood of the two men and ganged to watch. The ragged baby in the broken pram was the only one of the group finding anything of interest away from the scene of the bombsite. It pointed vainly at the tall sky and dribbled. 'Now come on, Swift. I know this has been . . .'

'No, Horsley. You don't know what this has been. You can have no idea of what this has been because if you did then you would have kept away. You're standing on a grave, man. This is sacred ground. There is blood in the earth. A good deal of blood. When they raised her body, you see, beneath it, the hole she left seemed to be full of water. But it wasn't water, it was blood. It had not seeped into the ground. It happens. The warden said he'd seen it before. The clay retained it. What do you make of that?'

'You're clearly distraught. I won't keep you . . .'

'Come on, you're a keen gardener. What do you make of it?'

'I really would have no idea.'

'Exactly. You're a profoundly tedious man, Horsley. Your neighbours think so. The customers at your oh so tidy shop think so. I expect even Mona thinks so — although I imagine she recognises a kindred spirit. You have no friends because you are dull. You have no insight into any mind but your own, but worse, you have no interest. Look after the old place for me, will you.'

Swift walked away without another word, leaving Horsley marooned like a captain on a bridge. The gang of children saw him and began blowing raspberries. Horsley's face turned puce; he unclasped his hands and sauntered back towards his house. Despite the humiliation he had, at least, foraged sufficient information to see him through dinner with Mona. With suitable embellishment he knew he could work it up into quite a tale for the saloon bar that evening. He watched the lone figure of

Swift turn the corner towards the underground. His feelings about him were mixed, but he couldn't entirely shake off the conviction that, of all his neighbours, Swift perhaps deserved to be bombed out more than most.

*

Powers, it seemed, had asked him a question. It appeared an offer had been made. Swift asked for it to be repeated.

'Buy you a drink. That's all. First night. Welcome sort of thing. Yes?'

'Go on, Mr Swift,' Mrs Miller urged. 'It'll do you good. Get you out of yourself.'

Despite the fact that Swift was as far out of himself as he would ever wish to be, he accepted.

They walked three abreast along the blackened street. The rain had started again and the swish of tyres on the wet road was the first they knew of each approaching cycle. Mrs Miller took Swift's arm to guide him over the unfamiliar terrain. She warned him of the approach of each kerb with a little gentle pressure on his elbow. Powers hummed tunelessly in the night, occasionally breaking off to shuffle a few dance steps on the pavement. He broke wind loudly. Swift took his cue from his landlady and ignored it. They turned a corner into the high street. As they passed a figure in a shop doorway, a torch clicked on and briefly illuminated a woman's face.

'Not tonight, love,' Powers said with a degree of compassion Swift found surprising. The torch was switched off and the prostitute was once more plunged into darkness.

Powers pushed first through the blackout curtain into the pub. The small bar was busy and thick with cigarette smoke; at the piano a drunk was picking out the notes of a popular song with one finger, his head propped on his other hand, elbow bent for support on the keyboard. There were no women in the bar and none of the men had removed their coats. They were drinking hard; there was little talk and no laughter. Powers elbowed his way quickly to the front and brought the tray of drinks back to the table. Swift saw that his attempts at drawing two of the men at the bar into conversation were met with stony-faced indifference.

'Cheers.' Powers raised his dripping pint and Swift and the woman clinked their glasses on his.

'You stayed with your sister then, did you?' Mrs Miller sipped her brown ale, keen to keep Powers from the subject of Swift's son.

'Yes. For a night. Then I . . . let me see. Yes, then I had a brief spell in hospital.'

'Don't tell me,' Powers said. 'You don't want to talk about it.'

'I don't mind.'

'What was wrong then?'

'I was confused. That's all.'

'What do you mean you were confused?'

A glass smashed at the piano; one of the men at the bar moved quickly to the drunk and supported him out to the street. The man went unprotesting, hat brim in hand, weaving across the floor. Without the music the mood lightened. Somebody laughed; the laugh became a harsh racking cough. His companion pummelled him enthusiastically on the back. Powers extemporised on the subject of confusion while the landlady sipped her ale, her mind somewhere else, and Swift struggled to remember exactly what had happened between leaving Dorothy's and arriving at the hospital.

'I was with my sister and Patrick. And their two boys. And ... one night — or morning it must have been — one morning. No, in fact it was the morning after I arrived, I decided to come back to London to find my ... yes, I set off and then ...'

'Yes?' Powers prompted.

'This is where it becomes confusing. You see at this point I find myself in a hospital. There's a gap.'

'You were knocked down!'

'No. I don't think so.'

Powers launched another solution. 'Bombed out then. That's right — you were bombed out and you lost your memory. Am I right?'

'No. As I said, there's something of a gap.'

'I'm not surprised you're confused, Mr Swift,' Mrs Miller offered.

'I get it!' Powers said. 'It was a nut house.'

'Yes,' Swift said, 'it was a nut house.'

'That's all right,' Mrs Miller said with a forgivingness that Swift found irritating.

'Told you, Joyce,' Powers exclaimed gleefully. 'I told you he was rum.'

'Oh, I'm sure Mr Swift had his reasons. Didn't you?'

'Reasons? I'm not sure . . .'

'Well there must be reasons.' Now the woman was looking to Powers for a way out of her own confusion.

'Course there were,' Powers gamely offered. 'He went mad. Stark staring. I told you, Joyce, didn't I!' Powers gleefully sipped his drink. Having found the weak spot in Swift's defence he knew now that all he had to do was to work on it to regain his former privileged position in the household.

'I imagine I did. Though it's a little hard to tell from the inside looking out.'

'Told you, Joyce. I told you he was rum.' Powers, having seized on the insight, was convinced that it bore repetition.

'Look, I'm sorry.' Swift stumbled to his feet; the beer and Powers' conversation had gone immediately to his head. 'I really ought to go to bed.'

'What's up?' Powers said. 'You confused again are you?'

'No. I really ought to go. I don't think this is a very good idea.'

'Short arms, long pockets, Joyce. That's what Swifty's got.'

166

'Go in through the back,' Mrs Miller said. 'The door's open. We won't disturb you if you want to get your head down.'

'Thank you.' Swift pushed his chair back under the table and lurched out of the room.

Outside he turned left. He had no clear idea of where he was going, but instinct led him back to the street of shops. The buildings around him lurched in and out of focus. The grim black squares of shut-up stores were locked tight so that no light spilled out and no life was allowed in. He paused by the doorway where the prostitute had accosted them. She stepped obediently from the shadows but did not turn on her torch.

'Who are you?' Swift said.

'That's none of your business, sir.'

'I want to see your face,' Swift whispered although there was no-one close enough to hear. The woman turned on the torch and turned it upwards so that her face was held like a ghost in the white triangle of light. She looked at him warily, waiting for his demands.

'You're very young.'

'Yes.'

'How much?'

'That depends on what you want, sir.'

'How much for all night?'

'That depends what you want, sir.'

'Here.' Swift thrust a pound note at the girl, she snatched it away from him. 'Now go home.'

He began to walk away, expecting her to strike off in the opposite direction. Instead the woman stepped back, waiting for the next footsteps on the wet pavement. He had no energy to pursue the matter.

*

Swift reached the front of the house then followed the terrace until it broke for the entrance to the back alley. He picked his way along the narrow rubbish-strewn track until he came to the back gate which he knew had not been closed since Powers' return. The smell of their meal and stale tobacco smoke hung in the kitchen. Swift took off his shoes and sat in the dark room warming his feet by the orange glow of the low fire. He wanted to be alone to remember; Powers and the woman had no right to his memories.

He tried to sleep but the seat was uncomfortable so he went upstairs. He had lost the habit of undressing and lay on the bed fully clothed. The ceiling spun with the drink; he sat up to fight the nausea but he was exhausted. He lay back again and slept.

He was woken by voices on the stairs. Powers and Mrs Miller were noisily negotiating their way to bed. Powers was making no effort to tone down his voice but it was the woman's voice that woke him: a sibilant 'shh' and stifled laughter cut through the darkness more sharply than Powers' drunken ramblings. Swift listened to two doors open and close then turned over and focused on the soft sweep of rain on the roofs and the slow gush of the gutters. But sleep would not come. He had a raging thirst and an urgent need to empty his bladder. He felt under the bed but couldn't find a pot so he put on his shoes and crept downstairs. The rain didn't trouble him on the short walk across the yard to the privy. He felt it seep into his scalp and run down his neck. He welcomed the cold and paused on his trip back to turn his face to the sky.

In the kitchen he filled a teacup with water and drank it greedily. He filled another, then he heard the door open behind him. He tensed and made a pact with himself. If it was Powers he would leave there and then, perhaps return to the rest centre, perhaps even return to Manchester.

'We woke you, didn't we?' Swift was relieved to hear the woman's voice, still thick with drink. She came into the room and sat at the kitchen table without turning on the light.

'Yes,' Swift said. 'Do you mind if I open the blackout?'

'No. I don't mind.'

He pulled back the black curtain and opened the window. The rain continued to sluice down the yard. He breathed in the cool fresh air.

'I like the rain,' the woman said, tugging her dressing-gown more tightly round her. 'I like the rain and the snow. I was born in November. They say you like the season you were born in.'

'Do they?'

'I'm sorry about Powers,' the woman said.

'I don't care about Powers. In fact I'd rather not think about him when I don't have to.'

'He means well.'

'Does he?'

'Well. You know. He's company, and I trust him. That's all you can hope for, isn't it?'

He took Powers' place at the table. In the imperfect darkness he could make out the shape of the woman opposite but he could not see her eyes.

'Why did you come here?' the woman said.

'I told you. I came to find my son.'

'Tell me the truth. I won't mind. I don't care what it is, I won't report you to the police.'

'It is the truth. I swear.'

A match scratched and flared. Swift saw a fleeting glimpse of the woman's scepticism before it burnt out.

'Why should I lie to you?'

'I don't know, Mr Swift. I don't know you well enough yet.' The hot coal of her cigarette glowed as she drew on it.

'It is the truth.'

'And your wife?'

'She died. In the raid. Didn't I tell you?'

'No. You mentioned your son. That's all.'

'Yes.'

'I had a friend who was bombed out — as well as Powers. I suppose we all do.'

'Go on,' Swift prompted.

'She was in the kitchen. Next thing she knew she heard this scratch — like somebody was scratching the sky but really close. She said it was like it was inside her head, then a rush and the air sort of falling apart. Then the ceiling came in, and she just fell and clung on to the carpet. She said it was like being dragged under the sea — just holding on to the carpet to stop being dragged under. That's what she said.'

'Was she hurt?'

'She couldn't hear for a day or so. But she never listened anyway so it didn't make a lot of difference. Haven't seen her for a few days. I wonder what she's doing.'

Swift helped himself to a cigarette. The woman's voice soothed him. Her whisper was pitched at a lower register. The huskiness was warm and welcoming, he wanted to hear more.

'Tell me more about your boys.'

'No. That's not fair. Every time I want to know something about you you turn it onto me. It's your turn.'

'Oh, I'm very . . . ordinary.'

'No you're not. You're not ordinary at all. Even if you were before . . . well, I think you grow through pain.'

'And pleasure?'

'No. Pleasure keeps you young. Now, come on, you're doing it again.'

'Would you mind if I didn't talk?'

'I might.'

'I find ... it's rather hard to explain ... I don't want to go back you see. The past is ... it's fragile ... and I want to be clear about it before I ...'

'Perhaps when you find your boy then.'

'Yes. Exactly. That's exactly right. When I find my son I think I'll feel more able to contemplate all that happened before this wretched war.'

'Is that why you went to the hospital?'

'Yes. I think that may be why I went there.'

THE HOSPITAL

SWIFT'S temples were being swabbed by a nurse. He could feel the methylated spirits cool his face as the liquid ran down to his ears. He was sitting in a wheelchair.

'There.' The woman discarded the ball of cotton-wool into a metal bin. 'Now. Do you wear false teeth?'

'Of what possible interest could that be to you?'

'We don't want you to swallow anything, Mr Smith. It's for your own good.'

'Swift. The name is Swift.'

The woman checked his notes for confirmation; it was clear she was not going to take his word for anything. 'Swift. Yes, so it is.'

They were in a small anteroom on the second floor of the building. The doctor's consulting room beside the cedar garden was next door, and beyond that another room and then the ward. Swift had come round in the ward after his attempted escape then been helped into the wheelchair. He was angry. As far as he was concerned, he was now suffering the double indignity of not only being prepared for a dose of the treatment but also being held against his wishes. He had not seen the nurse before, but he had already discounted the option of appealing to her better nature. Her starched cap and pristine uniform matched the formality of her behaviour towards him. She had no visible compassion; he felt that he might just as well be a corpse for post mortem for the care that was being shown to him. He longed for the tennis girl to appear. Although he had no faith in her being able to save him he wanted somebody there to empathise with him. And he needed someone he could trust when he came round to remind him of who he was, which is all he truly felt that he had left. The doctor walked in with one of his white-coated attendants. Recruitment of the attendants seemed to have been conducted solely on the grounds of height. None was shorter than six feet tall, and all affected a vagueness which seemed to Swift manifest in those who live looking down on the rest of the world.

'Good. All done then?' The doctor bristled with hand-wringing efficiency.

'Yes, doctor.' The nurse took this as a cue to leave.

'Splendid.' Fat Desmond lowered his bulk into the tubular steel-framed chair beside Swift's trolley and waved his attendant away like an unwanted courtier. Swift heard him stop in the corridor to stand sentry outside the door.

'I hope you don't expect me to be civil to you,' Swift said.

'I expect nothing. But I thought you'd appreciate the opportunity of venting your anger before the treatment.'

'That's most kind of you.'

'I think you'll be pleasantly surprised by the effect of it.'

'I doubt it.'

'What would you like to know? Ask me anything.' He threw his arms wide, tugging up his cuffs like a conjurer.

'I'd like to know why I'm being kept here against my will.'

'That won't be for much longer I assure you.'

'Then what do you intend to do with me?'

'I intend to interrupt the electrical pattern of your

brain for a fraction of a second by an electrical current. Seventy volts. This will induce a *grand mal* seizure.' The full horror of the statement was compounded by the smile with which it was delivered.

'I can't honestly say you're putting my mind at rest.'

'And I can honestly say that I am.' He smiled at his own witticism. 'Perhaps if I offer you some of the historical context . . .'

'Do whatever you like.' Swift wanted to hate the man but was being defeated by his reasonableness. The doctor was convinced he had good on his side which made him less odious but more dangerous; he was impervious to argument or criticism.

'It was pioneered by an Italian called Cerletti who experimented on pigs.'

'Really.'

'Yes. He followed some work done by a man called Meduna, but that's not important. What is significant is that he achieved remarkable results on a patient who came to him speaking gibberish. He was given one seventy-volt treatment for only one tenth of a second and the man burst into song. He then increased the dose and the man became lucid. The treatment has spread rapidly since then as a treatment for anything from acute melancholia to severe mania.'

'And how would you classify my condition?'

The doctor sidestepped the question. 'We're conversing, you're almost rational. It's progress, Mr

Swift, real progress. One more treatment and I think we can get you on your way.'

'More. You said "one more" treatment.'

'Yes I did.' His smile spread. He was enjoying delivering the surprise.

'So there have been others?' Swift voiced the question more for his own benefit than the doctor's.

'You don't imagine this is the first jolt we've given you, do you?'

'God.'

'Memory loss. I'm afraid it's one of the side effects. It's not necessarily permanent.'

'One of the side effects?'

'Yes. But I don't think we should dwell on those, should we.' The doctor walked out and his attendant came in and stood intimidatingly by the door. Swift knew he had to fight for time. He felt as though he was on the verge of real understanding. 'How long have I been here?' The attendant shrugged. 'It's important. How long have I been here?'

'A month. A year. I don't know.'

The nurse reappeared, released the brakes on the chair and propelled Swift out of the room. She backed through a set of swing doors and Swift watched a new corridor swim past. But it was not a new corridor. Fragments of his last visit and the visit before came back to him, his screams and shouts bouncing from the green walls. And the pressure on his wrists. He knew immediately that the last time he had been tied to the chair, and remembering that he remembered the procession of nurses he had been following, third in a line of chairs all moving towards the same room, like prams to a nursery, straining at the bonds on his wrists, twisting in his seat, being held down by heavy arms on his shoulders.

'I do wish you'd let me go.'

'It won't be long now.' The nurse addressed him like a child as she stopped by another door, opened it and wheeled Swift through. At the centre of the room was a bed beside a black metal box with two dials on the front and two electrodes trailing umbilically onto the bed. Behind the bed was a trolley with the sheets pulled down waiting like a coffin to receive him.

'Through here please.' Keen to maintain the momentum, the nurse helped him to his feet and opened a cubicle door to reveal a lavatory. She pushed him gently through and pulled the door shut behind him. 'Don't be long now, Mr Smith.'

Swift leant over the pan. He wanted to urinate but the fear was preventing him. He wanted to urinate like a child trying to please. He wanted to urinate so that they would be easier on him. He wanted to urinate so that they might permit him five more minutes to recall what he had known when he first entered that room. Because he now knew why he was there. It was Patrick who had found him, frantically digging in the allotment as the dawn rose and the light burnt behind his eyes.

He had been followed, he had intended to catch the milk train but felt drawn to return to the allotment. And it was Patrick who led him away and back to Dorothy who had looked at him and cried, then somebody had been fetched and he had pressed his point again and again that if he would only be allowed to dig then he could show them what was buried in the cold earth. Because it was too cold for life. Much too cold for life.

'All finished now?' The nurse swung the door open without waiting for his reply. While Swift had been in the lavatory the room had filled with people; four or five people, he really couldn't tell, all looking at him as though he was the most prized guest at a party. A tweed-suited man with copious grey hair was standing next to Desmond; clearly an observer, clearly someone of importance and power. They looked at him as though they were amazed that he could walk. He wanted to please, to walk round the room, to bask in their amazement; he was prepared to abase himself in any way they wished if only they'd let him be.

'This way.' He felt a hand at his back as he was eased onto the table and helped to lie flat. He looked up at Desmond, right up his nostrils, smelt his rank afternoon breath as someone tugged up his sleeve and injected him with something. Desmond was a reasonable man. His smile never faltered as he attended to his machine. The suited man watched him proudly; perhaps he was the owner of the machine, perhaps someone who had not seen it used before. He watched it with reverence as if he was waiting for a miracle.

Desmond whispered to the nurse. It was faint but Swift could just make out the words: 'Do you have the gag?' This is squeezed through an apologetic smile as if he has to play down the brutality for the man in the suit. The man in the suit smiles, he forgives Desmond, he has come to see the machine work, he would forgive Desmond anything. Swift feels the gag round his head, knotted at the back, his muscles already slack from the drug they have administered. Then he sees Desmond lean to the machine, turn a dial.

'Close your eyes,' the nurse implores him. It is the sole moment of humanity. Swift rebels, he keeps his eyes open. The four or five people in the room swarm over him. He feels their weight on his shoulders, on his legs, the man in the suit craning between them to see. Swift focuses on his face as Desmond attends to the machine. Something is slipped into his mouth. The dial is turned; in the split second before the floor opens and Swift falls through he sees Desmond look over his shoulder towards him. And in that moment he knows that Desmond has not the faintest idea of what he is doing. He watches like a child torturing an insect, abstractly appraising the pain of a species that is beneath his own. But the image of Desmond is snatched away as the floor falls and, though his body jolts and his teeth clash, and he screams out loud, he falls in on himself only to bounce back up screaming in a primal pain that twists his eyes towards each other to see the pain that the other is feeling.

Then it is over and the pause in his life is deeper than sleep. His mind has forced itself to go deeper to assess the damage the machine has caused it. It examines the bruises before it allows him to wake, which he does again on the bench beneath the cedar tree. The nurse has left him there. It is the second moment of humanity. And when he wakes he is first aware of his teeth. One of his front teeth is broken. Swift discovers this as he runs his tongue across it then tastes the grit in his mouth. He is unclear when he wakes where he is. The horror of the treatment has been obliterated by the treatment itself. He reaches with shaking hand for the water glass on the metal table beside his bench. He has an immense sense of well-being that he clearly remembers experiencing only as a child. The sun spreads over him, around him, cocoons him in its warmth. The tennis girl is watching him from a distance, sitting on the court sucking the long ribbon hanging from her straw hat.

'Hello,' the child says. 'Would you like to play tennis?'

'I'm hardly dressed for tennis.'

'Yes, you are.'

Swift looks down and sees that he is.

'Your eyes are terribly bloodshot. I suppose that's the treatment.'

'Yes. The treatment. Thank you.' The child, he knows, has read his mind. He is cured because he can now remember the treatment.

'I watched them.'

'Did you?'

'And I watched them bring you out here. I couldn't do anything to help you.'

'You have helped me.'

'I don't feel I have.'

'I have to go,' he says.

'To London. To find your son.'

'Yes . . . no.' The spell breaks and Swift remembers what he knew when he was digging in the allotment. He remembers what he knew when he was waiting in the church. He remembers what he felt as he walked to the village and the fear he experienced as he lay on the bed in the department store on the night of the raid. In remembering the treatment he also remembers the reason for it. 'My son is dead.'

'I know.'

'T HERE,' Swift said, 'that's all I know.' In the darkness of the kitchen the woman remained silent. He felt her hand on his, rough as pumice. 'I suppose I was cured. I mean, I suppose that's how they would see it.'

'And how do you see it?'

'I don't see it clearly at all. There are parts of my life I hardly remember now. I barely remember the funeral. I can recall the raid. Fragments. That's all. But it's coming back — slowly.'

'Just as well I suppose.'

'The digging. I only remembered that tonight. Patrick finding me. All that. It is returning. Perhaps you can understand why I'm so intolerant of Powers.'

'You don't need to explain. Powers rubs everyone up the wrong way.'

Swift knew he could sleep now. But he did not want to sleep alone. The pressure of the woman's hand was still on his, but because he could not see her face in the dark her intention was unclear. 'Why did you come here?' Her voice was soft as velvet with the concern she was showing him. Swift could hardly bear her sympathy.

'I came to find my son.'

'But your son is dead.'

'Yes.'

'Tell me. I want to help you.'

'I feel that I'm nearer to him here than anywhere else.'

'Yes.' Mrs Miller remembered the ghost shadows of her own boys bouncing on the bed, refusing sleep. The shiver of her fear for them as they slept huddled for warmth in the cold Welsh farmhouse.

'You see, as you go on, you go back. All the time: back and back.'

'You live in the past, you mean.'

'No. Everything is the past. It's simply . . . simply a matter of perspective, of significance, and the course you choose to plot between those moments. Do you see?'

'No. I'm sorry, I don't see.'

'It doesn't matter.'

'I'd like to understand.'

'It doesn't matter.' Swift felt his strength returning. There was somebody he knew would understand and he had her address securely folded on a scrap of paper in his wallet.

He went upstairs and packed his few belongings in Dorothy's bag then lay back on the bed and slept, clutching the bag for security to his chest. The dawn woke him. He left a week's rent on the kitchen table and let himself out before he had to face Powers again.

He walked from Battersea over the bridge towards Victoria, pausing to peer at a long barge passing the power station. The river was low; the wake from the boat washed at the rubbish scattered on the banks. A crane on the pier beside the power station swung low, unloading coal; the seagulls swooped at the barge packed with rubbish. Swift jumped onto the platform of a bus which took him to Victoria where he got off. Out of habit, he picked up a newspaper and rolled it beneath his arm. The station was busy, a few commuters were coming off a train from the suburbs, hurrying towards the bus platforms for the buses to the city and the West End, or striking out up Victoria Street towards Westminster. They were eager to start the day as soon as they could; days were too often curtailed by the raids. When the first alarms sounded it was a rush to make the train home before the city was paralysed.

Swift paused to unfold the address for the second time that morning. The flat was in Bloomsbury. He looked at it as though he was afraid it would disappear. He had memorised it but the small square of paper made it real enough for him to rely on it.

He walked past the palace and across the park to Piccadilly. A family emerged from the underground station carrying their rolled bedding beneath their arms. They looked tired, dishevelled and defeated.

The man nodded, Swift touched the brim of his hat. They both felt better for the exchange. From Regent Street to Bloomsbury Swift's mind was a blank. He was aware of people pushing past him, of glass being swept, of shops opening but he was remembering Pettigrew's face and the final farewell with the woman and Arnold on the train. He tried to recall how she had looked when she'd given him the address. At the time he knew he clearly felt that she wanted him to come to her, that the offer was of something more than simply a cup of tea. But he was afraid it might not extend to what he had now invested in it. Beyond reaching her flat he had no further thoughts, and he did not relish the prospect of the infinite choices open to him should she not be in.

Reaching Russell Square he found a café for breakfast. He was the first customer of the morning and waited as the woman behind the counter lit the gas on the stove, swilled the heavy pot with boiling water, took the chairs from the tables, wiped the counter and buttered the bread. She took it for granted that he was in no hurry and he was happy to sit cradling his tea and waiting for the day to begin.

He ate breakfast and the café filled. At a little after nine o'clock he took his case and left. The woman behind the counter watched him leave. In her judgment he seemed furtive, looking quickly around as though he was trying to make sure he wasn't being followed. He was the sort of person she felt she ought to bring to the attention of the police, but within a few minutes she had forgotten him. And when she did recall him later, when she had a moment to herself, it was because she remembered he'd seemed to be talking to himself, not glancing at the paper unrolled in front of him, just chatting silently to an imagined figure across the table. He had, though, a peculiar serenity about him, like a suicide waiting to jump. Knowing that the pain was all but over.

Swift found the building and walked into the stone-flagged hallway and past the cupboard of numbered brass letterboxes. He took the stairs to the first floor, then took another set to the next landing. Her name was written in bold black letters on a card within a small brass frame on the door, clean enough to indicate it had been recently done. Swift drew in his breath and then knocked. After a brief wait he knocked again, then heard someone inside calling for him to wait. He saw a shape approach through the misted glass at the top of the door. It paused, the blurred face peering at him, then the door was opened.

'Mr Bowler.' The matron greeted him as though she had been expecting him and Swift went in. She led him to the sitting-room, opening the curtains and inviting him to sit down. A gin bottle was open on the coffee table and, beside it, an empty glass and an open book. A rug was rumpled over the scuffed parquet; she kicked it flat. The tall-ceilinged room was sparse, with a wicker chair and an old two-seater sofa. There were a few paperback books strewn on a shelf, but the flat carried the air of a place recently, and hurriedly, abandoned.

'I should have let you know I was coming.' Swift was experiencing the first embarrassment he had felt in the woman's company.

'You look . . . tired.' She seemed unhappy with her assessment and continued staring at him as if he'd asked for her diagnosis. She had clearly just got up, her hair was uncombed, her face not made up.

'No. I'm quite well. Perhaps . . . perhaps a little tired.' He sat with his hat on his lap, his bag tight against his legs, rigid with formality. The woman continued staring at him, he met her look but couldn't hold it. She was stronger than he'd known her in the village, or perhaps it was he who was weaker. But she looked haggard and, Swift thought, a little drunk.

'I knew you'd come.'

'Did you?' Swift looked up defensively, immediately reading a criticism into her observation.

'Yes. It was only a matter of time, wasn't it . . . two lost souls. Who else are we to turn to?' She knelt on the floor and tipped a little gin into the glass. She held it up to the light through the grainy windows, then drained it. 'I think about it. All the time. The village. Do you remember what I said?'

'What? What in particular?'

'I said I thought we were dead. That we were walking through heaven.' She laughed. Hard. Like a drunk.

'Yes.'

'We were. The raid killed us both. At least it might just have well have done.'

Swift stood, quickly, picking up his bag. It was all wrong. He had given no real consideration as to why he was coming here. After all, he barely knew the woman, it was easy to mistake companionability for genuine affection. It was easy to blame the war, but so much of what he relied on was gone.

'Don't rush away, Mr Bowler. Please.' Still kneeling on the floor she lunged towards him, losing her balance, just catching herself with an outstretched arm from falling flat on the floor.

'No. No, I'm sorry. I have to . . .' He was at the sitting-room door. She viewed his embarrassment with a gentle mocking smile. It was clear he had misread her offer.

'Please. Wait.' She stood with difficulty and laid her hand on his arm. 'Please stay for a cup of tea.'

There it was. The final rejection. Swift did not want her tea. He did not want her gentle mockery. He wanted a home; a solution to his confusion; a reason he could build on to find his own reasons. He brushed her hand away, too roughly. He saw the familiar alarm in her eyes; he had attacked her before, she had no reason to expect that he wouldn't do so again.

He was in the hallway, caught in the web of confusion, looking out through the misted glass of the door towards the blur of the corridor. Somebody was walking past in a blue coat, leaving for work. He knew that if he left then he could never return. He saw her cloak on the coatstand, noticed details of the flaking paint, the stained paper, the scuffed parquet of the floor, the bare bulb in the ceiling.

'I do really think you should stay.' Even with the drink she was looking at him through nurse's eyes now, not wanting him to leave for his own sake rather than hers. But he knew little about her, she knew no more about him, how could she — he knew little enough about himself. The lines of communication between them were as tenuous as they had been when they had first met in the train. The woman put herself between him and the door, blocking his way, allowing him no option but to push her aside. She stood tight, reaching blind behind her, holding onto the handle of the door, waiting for the storm to pass, waiting for the moment when he would calm and apologise. But he pushed her harder, saw her alarm, pushed her harder still, swept his hand across her face, saw her face slap sideways against the wall. Without her, Swift knew he had nothing. With her he had less still. She tried to parry his blows then gave up and held her arms over her head. Each time he struck her he heard her thud against the door. She tried to scream but her screams were muffled. She crumpled to the floor; he tried to push her aside then dragged open the door. She looked up as he left. Her lip was cut, a bruise spreading across her cheek. There were tears in her eyes.

'Did you find your son?' she said, sober now.

Swift walked away towards the present without looking back.